I0596645

WHO CAN U TRUST?

Author Jerz Toston

Who Can U Trust

By: Jerz Toston

Cover Designed By: Jazzy Kitty Publishing

Logo Designs By: Andre M. Saunders

Editor: Anelda L. Attaway

ACKNOWLEDGMENTS

I want to First thank and give all praise to Allah (SWT) without Him none of this would be possible.

I want to tell my kids Kai, Meesh, Lil Jerz, Deivyan, Riya, and Ceer, I love yall until death of me.

To my sisters, Ericka, Felisha, and Nika.

To my bro, Pounds, my peeps on lockdown, free the jails Day-Day, Matim, and C-How; I got yall until they free yall.

To my bros from the 8 kill, Cllulo, Rupt, Hov, Big Head, Crumb, Cuz Mike, Frank White, and Hop Wiggz.

Mom Dukes, I did it again book two.

I can't forget my hair stylist Ms. Camper, love you Girl.

Thanks to Anelda the staff at Jazzy Kitty Publishing.

Lastly but not least, my better half, my soulmate Tambra, I know it has not been easy but you always have my back no matter what. My Bonnie to my Clyde.

DEDICATIONS

This book is dedicated to Mom Betty and Moe Good. I know yall are smiling down on me.

I Luv Yall!

TABLE OF CONTENTS

TABLE OF CONTENTS

INTRODUCTION

At the tender age of 10, Nafee witnessed his father gunned down in front of him by someone he thought was a friend so, he vowed to get revenge.

Cam who was Nafee's best friend had been stealing from him, but later went to jail and became envious of him.

Shelly was the love of Nafee's life and the mother of his son who crossed him in a way that was truly unforgivable.

So, now he had to ask himself a serious question. **Who Can U Trust?**

CHAPTER 1

Nafee Dreams about His Dad

"Nafee, Nafee..."

"Huh?"

"Wake up Baby it's time to get ready for school."

"I don't feel good Mommy."

"I told you if you take your butt to bed at night you wouldn't be tired every morning."

"But I don't feel good."

"Ok, if I take your temperature and you're not sick, you won't be having a birthday party this weekend."

I jumped up and ran into the bathroom to brush my teeth and wash my face.

"I knew that would make you change ya mind," my mom said from her bedroom.

When I got downstairs my mom had breakfast waiting on me as she always did.

"Nafee, you really need to start going to sleep at night."

"Mommy is hard, I even tried counting sheep."

"How hard could it be for a 11-year-old boy to fall asleep, especially after playing hard all day?"

"Truth is, ever since my dad was killed in front of me I've been having nightmares about it."

"Nafee are you still having those dreams?"

"No Mommy," I said lying so I wouldn't have to see that doctor anymore.

"Baby it's okay if you are, that's a normal thing. It's only been a year since it happened." I can still remember it like yesterday.

"Nafee you wanna take a ride wit me to get some ice cream."

"Yes Daddy, Yes!"

"Okay, okay, calm down its only ice cream."

"Samad don't let him eat that before he has his dinner."

"Calm down Cookie, I know tha deal."

"I'm just making sure and bring me some."

"I know, I know Butter Pecan."

We both gave my mom a kiss for leaving not knowing it would be the last time she got to kiss my dad, alive anyway. Like always we got the ice cream and an ice cream cone for us to eat before we left.

"Don't tell ya mom about this."

"I never do Daddy; do I?"

"That's my Boy."

"Aye Samad what it do Baby Boy?"

"I can't call it Ray-Ray."

"Yo I need a bird, you got me?"

"Ain't Shit jumping right now."

"Why you always runnin' that Bullshit on me?"

"It ain't no Bullshit, I won't be ready for a few hours."

"Nigga cut tha crap, if you don't wanna do bizness wit me just be a man and say it!"

"Look, I'm not having this conversation wit you right now in front of my son."

My dad turned to walk away and Ray-Ray pulled out a big gun which I later found out to be a .357 magnum.

"Daddy watch out!" *(BOOM, BOOM, BOOM)*

All 3 shots hit him in his back.

"Nigga don't you ever turn ya back on me!" Ray-Ray yelled, kicking my dad and his side.

"Stop, Stop Mafucka!" I yelled.

"Little Man I suggest you stay in a child's place," he said putting his gun in my face.

"I'm not scared of you," I said looking him in the eyes like my daddy said every man should do.

"Oh, you got balls too?"

My dad was trying to say something but started choking on his blood. *(BOOM)* Ray-Ray shot him in his forehead causing blood to gush out of my daddy's head.

"Aye Little Man when you get a little older you can come work for me."

"Fuck you Bitch!"

Ray-Ray smiled then walked back to his car. I sat there holding my dad in my arms waiting for the ambulance to come even though I knew he was already dead. I was in a state of shock by the time the police and paramedics arrived.

"Nafee, Nafee..."

"Huh?"

"What are you thinking about?"

"Daddy."

"I miss him too Baby."

"I better go so I won't be late for school."

I started out the door when my mom said, "Boy I know you better give ya momma a kiss."

I kissed her and then bolted out the door.

CHAPTER 2

Cam and The School Fight

"Cam get ya ass outta bed and get ready for school."

"A'ight, A'ight no need to yell."

"Boy who tha hell you talking to?"

I didn't say Shit, I just went into the bathroom and took care of my hygiene. Once I was done, I put on the clothes my mom had laid out which consisted of a pair of blue Polo jeans, white Polo button up and white shell top Adidas. My mom always made sure I was *"fresh to death"* especially since I was an only child and had no father around.

On the way, down stairs my mom said that my lunch money was on the Entertainment Stand and she would be home a little late. Whenever she worked late I would go over Nafee's house. He was my best friend, but we were more like brothers.

I put me a Toaster Strudel in the toaster since my mom didn't have time to cook me breakfast this morning.

"Baby, I gotta go, please make sure you lock tha door."

"Mom can I have some more money? Me and Naf wanted to go to tha arcade after school."

"Here take this 5 dollars."

"Thank you," I said kissing her on her cheek.

"Love you Cam."

"Love you too Mom."

She didn't know, but I was spending that on a nickel bag of weed after school. I decided to eat my food on my way to Naf's house.

CHAPTER 3

School

When I got there, he was just coming out the house.

"Damn, what were you in there doing?"

"Man, you know how my mom is."

"Nice kicks, my cousin got a pair of those."

"My mom bought them for me yesterday, I can change tha color of tha lotto's."

"My mom hit me wit $5 so it's on after school."

"My mom hit me wit tha same thing."

"We good then."

As we were walking to school this Black Caddy pulled up on the side of us.

"Yall want a ride?"

"Yeah!"

"Nah, we good," I said ice grilling the driver.

"Suit ya self then," he said pulling off.

"Man, why you do that?" I didn't say Shit I just kept waking.

"Do you know who that was? That's Ray-Ray, he has tha, city on smash."

"Fuck that Bitch Nigga!"

"What's up wit you and that Nigga?"

"I just don't like him."

"Well, I don't know about you, but I'm a run packs for him."

"No tha Fuck you not!"

"I want my own money so, I won't have to ask my mom all tha time."

"Well, if you start saving ya money you can buy ya own Shit."

"It'll take a whole year to save up to be able to buy a pack."

"All you need is 50 dollars."

"That ain't gon' get me Shit."

"Nigga it's a start."

"How you know so much anyway?"

"My dad put me down wit how much Shit should weigh and he even showed me how to cook it up."

"A'ight, so now all we need is tha 50 to get started."

"Unh, unh, I ain't doing that, my mom will kill me if she finds out."

"She's not going to find out though."

"I know cause I'm not doing it."

"Nigga you scared."

"No."

As we stepped in the door the bell rang.

"Right on time."

"I'll holla at you lunch time."

When I walked in my class I noticed we had a substitute teacher and she was fine as Shit.

"Excuse me, could everyone take their seat please?"

We all did as she asked except Titus who thought he was a Bad Ass.

"Did you hear what I said Mr. Titus?"

"How do you know my name?"

"Well let's see, you all have name tags on your desk and you're tha only one not seated." The whole class started laughing.

"Whoever is laughing can see me after school."

"Boy shut up and sit down, ain't nobody scared of you," said Shelly.

"Shelly don't make me smack you."

"I wish you would try."

"OK that's enough, Titus and Shelly sit down please." Titus was disrespectful to females.

"What you looking at Faggot?" I didn't know he was talking to me so I didn't respond.

"Does everyone have their assignment that was due today?" Everybody pulled out their paper.

"Today we're going to do something different we're going to read them out loud. Who wants to go first?" Shelly's hand went up first. When it was my turn I didn't want to read mines, not in front of the class anyway.

"I can't read."

"Yes, he can, he just don't want to," Shelly said with a big smile.

"He's a little retarded," Titus added causing a few people to laugh.

"Mind ya biz-ness wit that dinky sweater on." Everybody laughed, even the teacher smiled.

"Bet you won't say that after school Punk!

"Ain't nobody scared of you," I said standing up.

"Hey sit down Titus."

"He stood up first."

"You've been causing problems since you walked in, now sit down or you'll be going to Principal Bry's office."

"I'll see you after school Punk." When the bell rang for lunch I got up and headed to the door. Cam was already waiting outside when I got there.

"I'll see your Punk ass after school," Titus said brushing against me as he walked by.

"What tha Fuck was that all about Naf?"

"That Nigga was talking Shit so I let him know I wasn't scared of him."

"He can try something if he wants to."

"Cam I'm not worried about him, he's all talk."

The lunch hall was packed like always, but today the tension was so thick you could cut it with a knife. Titus was standing with his boys mean mugging me.

"I'm bout to go bust his ass right now."

"Nah Cam chill."

"A'ight he got that for now, but if he steps to you after school, I got him."

"Nah, if he really wanna fight Imma fight him." We ate lunch and then headed to class.

"Don't try to leave early."

"Look Titus if you really want to fight, meet me in tha park around tha corner cause I'm not getting suspended for kicking ya Ass."

"I'll be there, you just make sure you are.

For the rest of the day all I could hear were the words my dad would always say, *"Never let a man disrespect you because if he gets away with it the first time he'll think he can always do it."*

At 3 o'clock on the dot the bell rang. Cam was hyped up, he loved to fight. He was always the rowdy one, I was quiet and laid back.

As we got close to the park Cam said, "You better kick his Ass or Imma kick yours." *(Ha! Ha! Ha!)*

"What's so funny?"

"You."

"I'm not playing."

I had to laugh because I've seen Cam fight and I knew he was no match for me. I've been boxing since the age 5, my dad was a Golden Glove who trained me every day until he was killed and I still train every day. I couldn't believe all the people who were at the park when we got there.

"Damn, this is like a Tyson-Holyfield fight."

Shelly came up to me then let me know that she didn't want me to fight Titus and was hoping I didn't show up.

"Oh, you decided to show up."

I took my book bag off and threw my guard up. Titus threw a wild punch that I ducked and came back with a two piece of my own that stunned him, as well and busted his lip. He tried to throw a combination that I saw coming before he threw them. I wanted to laugh because his fighting skills were pathetic.

"Fuck him up Naf!" I heard Cam yell.

Next thing I knew Titus was charging me so, I sidestepped and caught him square on the chin knocking him out cold and just to show disrespect I spit in his face.

"Next time I won't take it easy on you."

"Yall got something yall want to say?" Cam asked his boys.

"Nah, it was a one on one."

"Damn Nigga, all these years' I thought you couldn't fight."

"I just choose not to."

"If I didn't know any better I'd swear you knew how to box tha way you threw those jabs."

I never told him I knew how to box because he'd want me to teach him and he has no patience what-so-ever.

"I never seen nobody get knocked out cold before."

"It's always tha first time for everything."

"I need to come up wit a way to get tha other 45 dollars."

"You're serious, ain't you?"

"Damn right, I'm tired of asking my mom for money every day."

"I'll show you how to bag it up, but I'm not messing wit it."

"Suit ya self, but don't try to jump on board when I blow up like Scarface."

CHAPTER 4

Happy Birthday Nafee

"Happy Birthday! Happy Birthday! Happy Birthday!" I woke up to and my mom singing and smothering me with kisses.

"Mom I haven't even brushed my teeth yet."

"Boy I carried you for…"

"I know, I know…9 months, 14 hours of labor and a split vagina."

"So, a little tart breath ain't gonna kill me."

"But I don't feel right Mom."

"Now you sound just like ya dad."

That brought a smile to my face. People always say I look just like my dad, but had my moms' good hair and gray eyes. My mom was 30, but didn't look a day over 23. A lot of people thought she was mixed because of her gray eyes and pretty long hair, but she was 100% Black.

"Nafee we're going to breakfast then shopping before your party."

When my dad was alive that's what we always did for my birthday every year. Rumor has it that my dad left my mom close to a million dollars. After I got dressed we headed to IHOP.

"Mom."

"Yes Baby."

"Can I ask you a question?"

"Sure, you can."

"Did Daddy leave you a million dollars?" She took her eyes off the road to look at me and then turned her attention back to the road.

"Nafee, your father did what he was doing to provide a better life for us and that he did." I knew it must have been true because she avoided the question.

"Even though I didn't want him in tha streets, I still held him down at all cost because that's what a real wife does for her husband, no matter what, your father knew that tha same streets he claimed would one day claim his life if he didn't get out. So, to answer ya question. No, your father did not leave me a million dollars, he left me 1.2 million."

I just sat there with my mouth open for a minute before I asked, "If Daddy left you that much money why do you still work?"

"Simple, if I stop working everyone would know he left tha money tha streets are talking about."

"I get it and by working they think it was all just rumors."

"Yup. We don't need nobody running up in our house looking for money that ain't there."

"Where you hide it…at Nana's?"

"No, it's in tha bank."

She went on to explain how they put it in the bank without alarming the feds; to say I was impressed would be an understatement. We ate breakfast and then did some shopping. My mom made me pick out something to wear to my party, so I picked out these Gucci sneaks with this Gucci V- neck and jeans. Since I told my mom I wanted a party with a DJ she rented out a hall from 5 to 10. I gave a lot of invitations out to kids in my school and from the neighborhood. My mom only allowed me to pass out a hundred, I didn't even know 100 people, but I still gave them out even though I knew they wouldn't all show-up.

"We better get home so you can get changed we can't have tha Birthday Boy showing up late for his own party."

I love my mom to death she always made sure I had the best of everything that's why I wasn't surprised when we got to the hall and there were balloons everywhere. Cam and Ms. Jonda were the first people to greet us.

"Happy Birthday Naf."

"Hey Birthday Boy give ya auntie a hug."

"Thank you for helping me out Jonda."

"You know I wouldn't miss this for tha world."

My mom and Cam's mom were best of friends and have been before either of us were born even thought of for that matter.

Shelly walked through the door with a gift in her hand and looking like one of Tyra's Next Top Model's with her Chanel dress and shoes on. Shelly always looked nice, but today she was flawless.

"Pick ya mouth up off the floor Naf," Cam said laughing, "you see her every day Shit."

"I know, but today she looks good as Shit."

"Nigga she looks like that every day, you just never paid attention to her."

Shelly was 5-5", caramel skin tone, a little round pump butt that was going to have niggaz going crazy when she got older.

"Now I normally play tha nice guy, but tonight Imma show you tha other side and grab you by ya neck try to make you wet it ain't workin' unless you sweat now."

"OOOOH this is my jam right here! Nafee let's dance."

Before I could say anything, Shelly had my hand leading me on the dance floor. I could tell by the way she was grinding her hips she wanted to do more than dance.

Wendy from around the way had Cam in the corner with her hands in his pants. All I could do was laugh. The party was in full swing when the lights came on.

"Mom what you doing?"

"Boy don't question me, I'm tha adult, not you."

Cam didn't say Shit because he knew she wouldn't hesitate to embarrass him in front of all the spectators. The D.J. cut the music.

"Let's all sing Happy Birthday to Nafee, and then yall can get back to partying."

As soon as they were done the DJ put on *'How Low Can You Go'* by Ludacris. All in All, my party was the Shit! I was sure they would be talking about it until somebody topped it. Shelly won the $50.00 my mom put up for the dance contest. I grabbed the mic and thanked everybody for showing up.

"Nafee do you think ya mom could give me a ride home? I don't know where my brother is."

"I'm sure she will, but let me ask her."

"Mom, do you think you can give Shelly a ride home? Her brother was suppose to pick her up, but he's not here."

"Sure. Come on Shelly," she said.

She gave my mom the address and off we went. We pulled up to this nice house where this lady was sitting on the porch.

"That's my mom."

"Oh, My God, Cookie is that you?"

"Porsha!" Shelly and I looked at each other baffled.

"Mom you know Shelly's mom?"

"Do I know her? Chile, they use to call us the 3-D's," Shelly's mom said with a big smile.

"Mom what does that stand for?" Shelly asked.

"The 3 Dimes."

"Who's the third?"

"Ms. Jonda," I said knowing the answer to that.

"Porsha, I thought you moved away?"

"I did, but I came back two years' ago."

"Let me give you my number."

"He looks just like Samad wit ya eyes and hair."

"Girl I know, he acts just like him too."

"Mom, I'm standing right here?"

"Boy I see you."

"Porsha make sure you call me so we can get together like old times."

"Matter Fact, what are you doing this weekend?"

"Nothing."

"We should all get together at my house to have a few drinks."

"Sounds good to me."

"Well, it's a date, I'll call you on Friday."

"A'ight."

"Bye Shelly, I'll see you in school Monday."

"Bye Nafee and Happy Birthday."

On the ride home, my mom explained how close the three of them were and that Porsha moved away to get away from Shelly's dad.

"If she moved away to get away from him, why did she come back?"

"Because he was killed two years' ago, in a botched robbery."

"Her dad tried to rob somebody?"

"No, they tried to rob him and when he didn't tell or show them where tha money was they killed him. I remembered my dad saying one of his workers were killed in a robbery."

"Mom was he one of Daddy's workers?"

"Yes why?"

"No reason, I just remember Daddy talking about it."

"So, you like Shelly huh?"

"Not like that, only as a friend."

"Well she seems to like you."

"I know she's always being nice to me in class."

"Well, not that it's any of my biz-ness, but I think you like her too."

"Mom!"

"I'm just saying, I seen you when she first walked into tha party; you were drooling all over ya self." *(Ha! Ha! Ha!)*

"Was not."

"Oh, yes you were."

"I was just amazed at how good she looked."

"Since Porsha is her mother, I know she looks like that all the time."

"Cam said tha same thing."

"Come on, help me take your presents inside."

I couldn't wait to see what Shelly got me; so, I opened her gift first. It was a nice Gucci shirt.

"What are you smiling at Mom?"

"Nothing."

"Yes, you are."

"Just that you made sure to open Shelly's gift first."

"You're making more out of it than it is Mom."

"If you say so; put this stuff away then get ya bath."

Once I showered, I went to bed and for the first time since my dad died I got a good night's sleep.

CHAPTER 5

Nafee and Cam Start Hustling

It was the first day of the summer and my mom trusted me enough to stay home by myself and not have to go to summer camp. I was getting dressed when I heard a knock on the door… *(KNOCK, KNOCK)*

"Who is it?!" I yelled coming down the steps.

"Nigga open tha door!" When I opened the door and Cam was sweating bullets.

"Damn Nigga, you sweating like a dog."

"It's 100 degrees out there."

"So, why didn't you just stay in tha house?"

"I need you to cook this quarter up for me."

I didn't want to be the bearer of bad news, but hustling wasn't for Cam. He's been hustling for 4 months and is only at a quarter, even after my birthday. I let him borrow $100 to get an eight ball, which I still haven't gotten back yet.

"Naf, can you stretch it into two this time?"

"Yeah but it's not going to be all that good."

"I don't care as long as I make 800." Fuck it, I had to let him know the truth even though I know he's not going to like it.

"Listen Cam, I don't think that hustling is for you."

"What you mean by that?"

"You've been doing this for 4 months and still haven't gotten anywhere, not to mention you still owe me a yard."

"Is this what this is about, the buck I owe you?"

"Nah, I just know by now you should at least be up to a big 8 (4½) and have some money put up."

"You think you can do better just cause ya dad taught you how to cook and weigh it."

"I never said that."

"Just cook my Shit so I can leave."

When I was done, Cam didn't say Shit, he just got his Shit and left. Cam never wanted to hear the truth so when he did he'd always get an attitude.

"Who tha fuck do he think he is to tell me hustling ain't for me. I'm tha one out here not him," Cam thought to himself.

When I got back to the Green Box I set up shop. Shit it's going pretty good, I was making money faster than I could count it, so I started stuffing it in my pockets wit out counting it. I had a smoker named Mr. Willy run for me.

"Little Man I hope you got a lot more, it's check day and it's gonna be like this all day."

"Mr. Willy, I'll be back in about an hour."

"Leave me a little something; something to hold me down til you get back."

I couldn't tell him no, all the money he was running despite the coke being booked up as he called it. After sorting and counting my money, I had a little over $900. I had enough to get an ounce and pay Naf his hundred I owed him. I made my way back to the eastside, grabbed what I needed then went back to Naf's house. Nobody answered the first time, I thought maybe he had left. I turned to walk away when I heard the door open.

"What was you doing?"

"Damn, can a nigga take a dump in peace."

"I didn't need to know all that."

"You asked what I was doing."

"I need you again," I said handing him the work I just brought.

"Where you get all this from?"

"Same place I got the last Shit. Here's ya money I owe you too. This time only make it 1½, Mr. Willy said the last batch was booked up."

"I could have told you that putting a quarter on a quarter. Tha only way you can do that is if tha work is raw fish scale and this Shit looks like it's already been stepped on. I wouldn't put nothing but a quarter on this."

He must have read my facial expression because he said, "You'll be making an extra 3 or 400."

"I wanna make all I can."

"True, but would you rather make more money wit Bullshit coke or double ya money with all oils? Cam tha thing is to have tha smokers come to you cause ya Shit is good and not cause ain't nobody else out but you."

"How do you know so much Naf?"

"My dad always schooled me in case I ever got in tha game."

"Well, why don't you come on board we can be partners 50/50."

"Only on one condition."

"I'm listening."

"You have to let me cook it my way and we have to do tha break off thing."

"That's two and what is the break off thing?"

"No more bags."

"Huh?"

"Listen, when you do bags you can't take shorts because you want $10 a bag, wit break off we can take it all from a dollar on up. Trust me on this Cam Imma show you why my dad was the man."

"A'ight if you say so.

"Nah Nigga, I know."

"So, we bout to get paid!"

There's only one problem

"What's that?"

"We need a bigger plug; this Shit is garbage."

"We could holla at Ray-Ray."

"No!"

"Damn, why you don't like Ray-Ray?"

"I just don't."

"Well then, we gotta keep dealing with them Cats from tha east."

"Hold up, I got an ideal," I said picking up the phone.

"Who you calling?"

I put my finger up to say hold up when the other end picks up, "Hey Uncle Kev." Cam looked at me like I lost my mind.

"What up nephew?"

"Do you remember when you said if I needed anything to call?"

"Yeah."

"Well, I need to talk to you face to face."

"A'ight, but you gotta give me a few hours, I'm taking care of some Shit right now."

"It's 10 o'clock," I said looking at my watch, "I'll hit ya phone at 4 o'clock sharp.

"A'ight, sounding like ya pop."

"Nigga is you crazy?"

"We can trust him, he won't tell my mom."

Kev was my dad's best friend, that's why I didn't understand why he didn't avenge my dad's death at first. I later found out that he was Ray-Ray's uncle and instead of killing him, he disowned him. I made sure to clean up everything so my mom wouldn't suspect anything.

"Come on Naf, let's go get this money."

By the time, we got to the Green Box, Mr. Willy had the smokers lined up around the corner.

"Damn Young Buck, I was about to take them somewhere else."

"I told you I'd be back, I had to get my brother."

"Well, this guy needs 4, she needs 6, he wants 8."

"Hold up, hold up," I said, "just tell me how much money they got."

"I got 40," one man said. I broke him off a piece that was worth $40.

"Whoa what's this Young Buck?"

"40 dollars' worth of cocaine."

"What happen to tha bags?"

"Ain't no more bags, just break off."

"Well, I got another $11 for you." I broke him off another little piece.

"If it's good, I'll be back."

"We'll be here," I said knowing he'd be back.

It wasn't the best coke, but it was a lot better than the other Shit Cam sold them.

Around 3:30 pm it slowed down. We were just about done anyway. So, we hit Mr. Willy and let him know we would be back in the morning.

"Nah Young Bucks you have to come back about 6 o'clock for the next rush."

I thought about it and then said, "A'ight, we'll be back at 6, but we can only stay til 10 o'clock."

"That's cool." Cam wanted to know how we're going to pull it off.

"Easy we don't have to be in til 10 o'clock so we'll just trap til then."

We had made 1800 off that and still had a quarter left. I called Kev exactly at 4 o'clock.

"I swear you're just like ya dad; I'm pulling up anyway. Damn Little Nigga, you got big since the last time I saw you."

"That was only 6 months ago."

"So, what's on your mind?"

"First you gotta promise this stays between the three of us."

"Uh oh, this must be serious."

"Me and Cam want to buy some weight."

"Ha! Ha! Ha!" When he saw, I wasn't laughing he asked me if I was serious.

"Yeah I'm serious."

"You don't know tha first thing about hustling."

"Uncle Kev my dad schooled me on tha game."

"Let me ask you a few things. How many ounces in a big eight?"

"4½"

"How many grams in a half brick?"

"504."

"Do you know how to cook coke?"

"Yes."

"What's the best way to cook it?"

"Dry cook it and by that, I mean to use less water as possible." When he smiled, I knew I had him.

"Samad has taught you well and if I'm as smart as I think I am, you be runnin' this city by tha time you hit 16."

"So, does that mean you'll be our supplier?"

"Yes, but if Cookie finds out my name stays out of it."

"No problem."

"You don't keep no drugs or money here."

"Where am I supposed to keep it?" He threw me a key.

"This is a house ya dad had; I knew it would come in handy for something."

"Where is it?"

"On tha west side."

After he gave me the address he asked me if my dad taught me how to drive

"Yes."

"I'll have my peeps up my way make you a fake license so you can get back and forth."

"Cam needs one too."

"I got it covered. Tha funny thing in all this is that Samad made me promise if anything would happen to him to make sure you and Cookie were straight. He also said that if you got into tha game make sure you were straight. I knew you would probably start, just not this soon."

"Uncle, I'm tired of asking my mom for things."

"How are you gonna explain things when the money starts coming in?"

"You."

"Ha! Ha! Ha! Just like ya dad quick on ya feet. One more question, suppose I said no and told Cookie?"

"I would have denied it and said I wanted to see if you really had my best interest."

"Damn Naf you good; Samad has definitely taught you well. So, how much do you want me to front you?"

"Nothing, we just want what our money can pay for."

"How much you got?"

"3800." Cam looked at me like I was crazy.

"For another 400, I'll give you 6 ounces."

"A'ight," I said running to my room to get the money.

"Naf, you know I live in Philly so I'm not going to be running up and down the highway for a few ounces."

"It'll be worth it." Cam asked if the work was good.

"It's tha best you'll find on the east coast." That brought a smile on my face.

"I got 6 ounces in tha car." When he was about to get up, my mom walked in.

"I thought that was ya car out there."

"Yeah, I came down to scoop nephew for a few hours."

"As long as you have my baby home by midnight."

"Not a problem."

"Cam call ya mom, see if it's OK if you can hang out wit us," Kev said.

Cam picked up the phone then hung it up as quickly as he picked it up.

"She said yes and to tell you hi." Kev ended up giving us a ride to the crib he's just given me.

"Don't worry about tha bills, I got them covered. Go ahead do that, so I can give you a ride back across town."

I ended up turning 6 into 8. We took 4 and left the other 4 for the morning.

"Yall be safe and I'll have that plastic by tha time ya call me."

"Kev, you got some heat for us?"

"Yeah, but take this for now," he said handing Cam a .380.

It was a little after 6 o'clock when Mr. Willy showed up.

"Listen Mr. Willy, if you're going to be on the team you need to be on time. Here, go try this out, this is what it is from now on." A couple of smokers came while Mr. Willy was gone.

"Hey Youngin, is this the same Shit from earlier?"

"Nah, this way better."

"You sure? Cause what you had earlier was real good."

"Well, it ain't got nothing on this."

"Well, I only got $6 for now."

"Here," I said breaking her off a 6-dollar hit.

"Thank you, Baby."

Mr. Willy came back, "Where did you get this Shit from?"

"You don't like it?"

"Hell Yeah! We gonna make a lot of money, I mean yall gonna make a lot of money especially if it's consistent."

"You said it right, we gonna make a lot of money."

"Young Bucks I ain't had no cocaine this good since late 70's. If you two Young Bucks keep this up you'll be kings of the city in no time, mark my words. Let me do what I do and get this money rolling." The time flew by and before we knew it; it was 11:30.

"We better pack up for tha night. I know we still have to run to the spot to put this money up. Mr. Willy, we gotta go, but will be back at 8 tomorrow morning."

"Yall not in trouble for staying out past 10 are yall?"

"No, we cool."

"This is for you," I said giving him a nice 40 piece.

"You Young Bucks sure know how to put a smile on an old man's face."

"8 o'clock," I said before we stepped off. We caught a hacker and made him wait around the block why we handled business.

"We need to call Kev, there's only an ounce left."

"Shit we ran through 8 ounces that fast." Let's count this money up and then call Kev.

"Wheeeeew! We're rich!" Cam yelled.

"Nigga calm down, this is only 14 Grand, this aint Shit!"

"Maybe not to you, but we made that in 5 ½ hours."

"Let me see that phone."

(After 5 rings, he picked up) "Yo."

"Unc can you come through wit 20 before 8?"

"Yall done that already?"

"All except one and we got enough for a half plus two."

"I'll be by at 7 and you got 10 minutes to get home."

"I know bye."

The hacker was still waiting. "Sorry we took so long."

"Don't worry I left tha meter on."

"Cam be up by 7."

"I'll be up."

"We need to get cell phones tomorrow, so tell ya mom Kev is buying us phones tomorrow."

"Gotcha!" he said running down the block to his house.

"I'm glad to see you still know how to get home."

"Mom its only 12:01."

"I know, but you my Baby, I'm allowed to worry about you."

"Yeah, but I was in good hands wit Uncle Kev."

"He's coming to get us in tha morning, and he's buying us cell phones tomorrow as a late birthday present...Mom"

"Yes, Baby."

"I really had fun today with Uncle Kev."

"I'm glad you did."

I took a shower and went straight to bed.

CHAPTER 6

The Come Up

My alarm went off at 6 o'clock.

"Nafee are you up?"

"Yes Mom...Kev called he said he'd be a few minutes late, but he'll be here. He said that me and Cam can work in his store for tha rest of tha summer to earn some money."

"I know he explained it all to me."

"I better call Cam and make sure he's up."

"I already did and I let Jonda know what you two would be doing for tha remainder of tha summer." I got dressed, ate breakfast, and waited for Kev to come.

"I got to go; make sure you lock up and turn tha alarm on when you leave."

"I will."

"Give me a kiss before I go."

"Love you Mom."

"Love you too. Oh, when you get your phone call me so I can have tha number." Cam was coming in as my mom was going out.

"My mom bought tha working in tha store story."

"So, did mines."

"That means we get to trap til 12 every night."

"Yeah, but don't think we're going to make 14 Grand a night either."

"Why not? You heard what Mr. Willy said about the coke."

"Yeah, and I also know it was check day too."

(Beep, Beep) "Let's go that's Uncle Kev."

"Good morning yall."

"Good morning."

"Sorry I'm a little late."

"It's cool this time, but make it tha last." Cam looked at me like I was crazy.

"Ha! Ha! Ha! Naf I swear you're your father's son. Punctuality was his biggest thing and truthfully I wanted to see if it was yours too."

"Uncle Kev I think we're being tailed, that car has been following us since we pulled off."

"Observant, another one of Samad's traits."

"That's my people."

When we got to the house it was 7:15, we had 45 minutes until we had to meet Mr. Willy.

"I don't mean to be rude, but here's the doe where's tha work?"

"What's the rush?"

"I have to meet somebody in 45 minutes."

He picked up his phone and told whoever was in the car to bring that inside. The dude that came looked like he was about 19. He handed Uncle Kev a black duffel bag.

"There's 20 ounces and two guns in in there."

"A'ight, I'll hit you when I'm done

"Hold up not so fast, these are the license I had done for yall and here's tha keys to the car outside. Come on let me show you how to use tha stash spot. This car is tagged up for 2 years' and the insurance is also paid up for 2 years."

After he showed us how to work the stash spot, he let us know how much we could put in it.

"Is it dog proof?"

"Yeah, trust me; I also left tha Philly tags on it since ya license is Philly. Don't be joy riding, this is just to get back and forth to the crib."

"I need to start cooking this up."

"A'ight, yall be safe and call me if you need me for anything."

I didn't want to be late so I decided to cook 10 which I turned into 14 oils.

"Young Bucks yall late; 8 o'clock means 8 o'clock." Even though we were only 5 minutes late he was right.

"Here's a little something to get you started."

"Nah I'm cool, I'm not getting high today."

Mr. Willy wasn't the average smoker, he always kept himself up and some days he wouldn't get high, like today. I knew that later on down the line Mr. Willy would be an asset and not a liability. What we didn't know was Mr. Willy rarely got high, he would sell the coke we gave him to pay his bills and buy nice clothes. I didn't find this out until the end of the summer.

"Cam, I know you don't have that strap on you?"

"You Damn right I do, I'm not going to let a nigga catch us slippin."

"What if tha Po-Po run down on us? What if a jacker run down on us?"

"I feel you but I'd rather take a loss than have you catch a gun charge."

"Naf they gonna have to catch me to charge me and I know these projects like tha back of my hand."

"Look how bout you just sit over there in tha cut and watch my back then?"

"A'ight, but if anything, even looks funny I'm coming out blazin."

"Be easy John Wayne."

"What ever, you heard what I said." From that moment, I knew that putting a pistol in his hand was a bad mistake.

"Young Buck let me borrow ya ear for a minute."

"What's up Mr. Willy?"

"You've been out here for about a month now."

"Yeah."

"I hope you are saving ya money."

"Now you insulting me Mr. Willy."

"I don't mean to, I just been around a long time and you definitely seem like you've been taught well."

"My dad kept me up on everything."

"Oh yeah, if you don't mind me askin' who's ya dad?"

"Samad."

"Holy Shit!"

"I should've seen tha similarities. Boy ya dad was a real Mafucka believe it or not but I use to run for ya dad. So, Cookie ya mom?"

"Yup."

"She's gonna kill you if she finds out you out here hustling."

"She's not, so I don't have to worry about that," I said more telling him than asking him.

"You don't have to worry about me saying Shit."

"Mr. Willy why do you get high?"

"Ha! Ha! Ha!"

"What's so funny"

"Young Buck do I look like a smoker?"

"No."

"Because I'm not, all tha coke you give me I sell it. Now don't get me wrong, I might lace me a blunt here and there, but that's as far as it goes."

"You just earned a spot on my team."

"I thought I was already on tha team Young Buck?"

"You were but now you just got a promotion. You can still run but I need you to hold it down after we go in."

"I can do that."

"Plus, school will be back in another month, so Imma need you to hold it down while we in school."

"No problem since this is my only source of income. I can't believe Samad is ya dad. Sorry about what happened to him, tha streets ain't been tha same since that punk Ray-Ray took over. Just tha mention of his name sets me off; Ray-Ray better enjoy his run cause it's about to be over."

It was 11 o'clock and dark as Shit since Cam shot the street light out.

"You can make this easy or hard; tha choice is yours."

"Cam stop playing."

"How ya know it was me?"

"Nigga I know ya voice."

"Suppose it was somebody else; you would've been robbed or even shot."

"That's why your over there in tha cut."

"I know but I still think you should have a piece on you."

"I can't take that risk, but I will put it over there."

"What good is it gonna do over there?"

"If a nigga want it, I'll walk them to it."

"Right, I Gotcha!"

For the next few weeks it was pretty much the same; money, money, money. We had two weeks before school started back; Uncle Kev took us shopping but we spent our own money.

"You two Little Niggaz made a lot of money this summer, so I decided to reward yall wit these," he said handing us both a jewelry box.

"Now this what I'm talkin' bout," Cam said smiling.

"Don't worry about Cookie or Jonda, they said it was ok for me to give yall these." We both had necklaces with our initials in ice.

"These look like they cost a couple ones."

"Nothing Major." I made a mental note to holla at Cam.

"This is enough stuff to last yall til Christmas." Cam went into U.S.A. Boutique, while we walked to Dr. Denim.

"Listen Naf, I loved ya dad like a brother and I told him that if anything ever happened to him I would always make sure you were okay. Ya dad never wanted this life for you, but he knew you would choose it."

"Uncle Kev I didn't want to get involved, but Cam isn't cut out for this game."

"I've observed tha way he sits in tha cut while you off tha work."

"How do you…"

"That's not important Naf, but understand this, he will protect you at all cost."

"He's cut out to do just what he's doing, watching and protecting you. Now don't get me wrong by no way is he a flunky, he's a shooter."

"That can be a good thing or a bad thing."

"I will say this, I would never want to cross him and be on tha other side of his gun."

"Unc, I feel tha same way about Cam that you felt about my dad."

"I know and I also want you to know that I couldn't kill my only sister's son because it would send her to her grave. I told him tha minute she dies, so does he."

That made me smile, I knew it had to be a reason he didn't kill him besides the fact he was his uncle. I remember my dad said that his sister was real sick. I knew that eventually Naf and Ray-Ray would bump heads at the rate Naf was going. It was only just a matter of time.

"Naf, I brought these Cartier Frames for you."

"We need to get back there's money to be made."

"Relax, Mr. Willy can handle it while we're gone."

"I know but I'm going to call him just to make sure he's OK." I caught Uncle Kev smiling out the corner of my eye.

"Mr. Willy is everything good wit you? A'ight let me know if you start to run low before I get back."

"Is everything cool?"

"Yeah."

"I told you that."

"Doesn't hurt to make sure. Uncle Kev let him know you always gotta make sure ya workers are straight."

"I wish I had workers when I was 12, must be nice." We went to lunch then Uncle Kev dropped us back off.

CHAPTER 7

Ray-Ray

"Mafucka, didn't I tell you not to play wit my Fuckin' money?!"

"You know I would never play with ya money Ray-Ray."

(SMACK) "Aaah Shit!" *(SMACK)*

"Nigga shut up! Now where is tha rest of my money!"

"I told you I have to bump tha rest of tha work."

"Why didn't you just say that then?"

"I did."

"Damn Jimmy, why you let me do that to him if he said he had to finish tha work?"

"I tried too, but you was in a zone."

"Damn, I gotta stop Fuckin' wit them dippers."

"I think that's a good ideal."

"Nigga Fuck You!

"Ha! Ha! Ha! Nigga you was really trippin."

"Man, tha boy Philly got that Shit."

"Kenny don't worry about that stack this one is on me."

"Faggot Ass nigga wasn't getting paid anyway; he lucky I didn't have my pistol on me."

"I'll have Jimmy drop something off to you later tonight.

"That's What's up," I said but really was thinking Fuck You Bitch Nigga.

"Ray-Ray was already over charging me, I swear if Samad was still alive, I wouldn't be broke or going through this Bullshit. As soon as I find another plug I'm gone!"

"Jimmy just make sure you hit me first so I can be around."

"Little nigga you just make sure you got ya Punk Ass around."

"I knew Jimmy was a Bitch, he only had heart when he was holding."

"What nigga, did I say something wrong?" I didn't respond, I just walked out the door with murder in my eyes.

"Ray-Ray I think we should cut that Mafucka off, ain't like he bringing or spending a lot of money anyway."

"I was thinking tha same thing."

"Well it's settled, he's cut off."

"What's up wit them niggaz from eastside?

"Shit, I'm glad you said something, I need to drop 2 bricks and 4 logs off to them."

"Come on let's make it happen I gotta drop some Shit off on tha hill anyway."

"Jimmy I feel good; I'm young, rich, look good and in tha best shape of my life."

"You something else."

"Ya Uncle Kev still not speaking to you?"

"Fuck that Mafucka!"

"I was just asking."

"He chose that Nigga Samad over his own flesh and blood."

"That was his right hand, I respect tha fact that he did that instead of sending you to tha boneyard."

"Nigga you sound stupid you must of had a dipper."

"Nah, on some real Shit, me and you been boys since tha sandbox, right?"

"Yeah and?"

"If ya nephew earthed me, what would you do?"

"I don't have no nephew."

"If you did."

"Truthfully, I don't know."

"Well, if it was me, I don't think I'd be able to kill my blood, so I would just stop Fuckin' wit him." I did see his point, but I would never tell him he was right.

"So, did you watch tha Super bowl last night?"

"Yeah, my Saints beat that Ass."

"So now you a Saints fan?"

"You know all my family is from New Orleans."

"Oh Shit, slow up."

"Damn, now you got me feeling like a stalker."

"I don't know why."

"I hit you wit my number and you never called."

"I told you I wasn't calling."

"You must don't know who I am!"

"I do, some nigga that thinks cause he got a couple ones he can get any chick he wants."

"So, you do know me," I said smiling.

"That Shit might work on them chicken heads but not me." She just shook her head and got in her car.

"Man, I don't know why you keep wasting ya time wit that young Bitch. She's only 2 years' younger than me plus, she seems independent. You know I like a challenge."

"You might be fighting a losing battle on this one."

"How much you wanna put on it?"

"I'll take that bet only on one condition."

"I'm listening."

"60 days."

"What?"

"You have 60 days to bag her."

"Bet."

"5 stacks is tha bet."

"It's still a bet, but I'm so confident I'll bet 10 stacks."

"This is going to be tha easiest 10 stacks I've won."

"Yeah, I think I'm gonna go to Vegas courtesy of Jimmy."

"Nigga, you don't even know her name."

"Excuse me."

"Yeah."

"Was that Zina you was just talkin' to?"

"Yeah it was."

"Damn, I told yall that was her."

"You know her?"

"Yeah, that's my sister and she was suppose to give me money to go to tha mall."

"If you don't mind me askin' what were you getting from tha mall?"

"A pair of sneakers."

"Here," I said pulling out my money and peeling off 3 crisp hundred dollar bills."

"Oooooh thank you."

"Shawty can you give her this," I said writing my number on another hundred knowing she would give her the number, but not the money.

"Now, what was you saying about me not knowing Zina's name?"

"That's about all you gonna get is her name."

"Holla at me in 60 days."

No soon as we dropped off the work we were being pulled over.

"License, registration, and insurance please."

"If it isn't tha one and only Detective Spiken. So, what do we owe this visit?"

"I believe you owe me something, don't you?"

"Last I checked, we good til next month."

"That would only be good if you took care of biz-ness this month."

"Jimmy, didn't you hit him?"

"Nah, I thought you did."

"Fuck, my bag Spiken."

"It's cool, just put an extra stack wit it for late fee's."

"Here's 6 for this month and next."

"Now see Ray-Ray that's why I like you cause you pay tha cost to be tha boss."

"What ever Nigga."

"Just leave tha money on tha seat, I'll get it while I search this pretty truck of yours."

"Come on Spiken."

"Mafucka shut tha Fuck up and get out! This only gonna take a few minutes.

"I hope so I got Shit to do."

"If you would've paid on time, we wouldn't be going through this dumb Shit."

After 5 minutes, we were allowed to get back in and leave.

"I swear, if that Mafucka wasn't an asset, I would've been sent him to his Maker."

"That was my fault, I thought you had hit him."

"It aint bout Shit."

"We had to give that Cracker extra money."

"Yeah, but that's tha price we pay to keep tha jakes off our back, so it's money well spent."

CHAPTER 8

Back to School

"Shelly, make sure you come straight home, Nana and Pop Pop are coming by."

"Ok Mom, love you."

"Love you too Baby."

I couldn't wait to get to school to see Nafee especially since I hadn't seen him all summer because he was working. Kamil and Shalil were the first people I seen when I got into school.

"Hey yall."

"Hey Shelly."

"Hey Shell, you look really nice."

"Is that dress Gucci?"

"But of course," I said in my British accent.

"Look at yall with yall Prada dresses on."

Kamil and Shalil were twins and my best friends. I didn't see them this summer because they went to stay with their dad. We had 10 minutes before the bell rang, so we caught up on each other lives over the summer.

"Girl is that Titus over there?"

"Mmm Hmm."

"He looks like he stepped his game up this year."

"I hope so, cause girl…" Cam and Nafee came walking in and all eyes were definitely on them.

"Look at Cam with his Sexy Ass," Kamil said.

"Fuck Cam, look at Nafee."

"Unh, Unh, Unh they blinging wit them chains on."

Nafee did look good with his True Religion Jeans and V-neck shirt.

"Hey Shelly, Mil, Lil, yall ready to start tha school year?"

"Yeah, I want it to be over already so I can start high school."

"Ooh me too, I know there are a lot of cute boys."

"There are cute boys here," Cam said, "well at least two anyway." We all started laughing when the bell rang.

I pulled my schedule out to see where my homeroom was. It just so happens we were all in the same homeroom including Titus.

"Everybody please be seated while I take roll call. When you hear ya name just say here or present."

Once that was done we were free to talk until the bell rang. It turned out me, Cam, Shelly, and Kamil were in all the same classes except one. When the bell rang for lunch I couldn't wait to get to the cafeteria to get some of those soft cookies.

"Nafee, can I holla at you for a second?"

"Yeah, Cam go ahead, I'll catch up."

"Nah, Imma wait right here."

"It's cool, he can stay."

"What's that all about?" Mil asked referring to Cam, Titus and Nafee talking.

"I don't know, but I'm sure it's nothing."

"Look, I've been doing a little hustling this summer and judging by those pieces around ya neck, so have yall."

"I got this spot over 25th I just need a plug."

"I haven't been on tha grind, my uncle got these for us."

"How much you coppin?" Cam cut in and asked.

"Only 3 to 4½ ounces."

"At what price?"

"4,050."

"It's not like we know anybody to turn him on to, so it doesn't matter, right?"

"Maybe Unc can help him out."

"I don't want no parts of it."

"Titus let me holla at my uncle and I'll get wit you by tha week."

"A'ight, good looking out."

"Cam, what tha Fuck you thinking about?"

"Expanding tha biz-ness plus selling a little weight."

"We don't need to do either of those things yet."

"Don't forget a few months ago, you didn't even want to get involved in this game."

"Yeah, but don't forget how much money we have made since I decided to help you out." I could see this was going to end up ugly so I defused the situation.

I said, "Look all I'm sayin' is Titus has a big mouth."

"Fuck it then, we won't deal wit him."

"Thank you."

Naf had no ideal, but I was gonna get this money and start saving up on the side. By the end of the day, I was more than ready to leave.

"Hey Nafee, is it a'ight if I walk home wit yall?"

"That's up to you."

"I seen you talkin' to Titus; yall cool now?"

"He was just letting me know there weren't any hard feelings."

"I would say tha same thing if I got my Ass kicked like that to."

"I respect that he even came to me."

"Well, he looks like he's into something."

"Why you say that?"

"Let's see, black labeled jeans & shirt, ACG Boots; need I say more?"

"Shelly, it is tha first day of school."

"Last year he wasn't dressed wit new clothes."

"So, what if he is into something, that's his biz-ness!"

"Shut up Cam, I wasn't talkin' to you."

"Shut up Cam, ain't nobody talkin' to you," he said mocking her. *(Ha! Ha! Ha!).*

"Just for that Imma tell Kamil not to holla at you."

"Oh, she's feeling a nigga?"

"Don't worry about it."

"Well, Imma tell Naf not to holla at you then."

"Boy, I don't like Naf."

"Yeah, what ever, tell that to somebody who might believe it or you."

"Nafee, tell him I don't like you."

"He doesn't know if you like him or not."

"Cam chill, she don't like me."

"Yeah a'ight, but if I don't know Shit else; I know about Bitches."

"Who you calling a Bitch?" Shelly asked while punching Cam in his arm.

"Oww, I wasn't calling you a Bitch and if you punch me like that again you'll be tha first girl I ever knocked out."

"I wish you would try it."

"Hey, let's stop at Mr. Benny's so I can get me a Blazing Hot."

"Boy get out of my head, I was thinking tha same thing."

"You know what they say, great minds think alike."

"Awe ain't that cute."

"Cut tha dumb Shit Cam."

"I'm just saying, it's obvious you two like each other; even a blind man would be able to see that." We both looked at one another, but said nothing.

"What tha deal Young Buck?"

"Just finished my homework."

"When I was in school they didn't give us homework on tha first day."

"Yeah, that was 20 years' ago."

"Imma need some more Shit, I'm just about finished."

"I'll make sure you good before I roll out."

"Young Buck I appreciate all that you've done for me these past months."

"Mr. Willy, I'm tha one who should be thanking you."

"If ya dad was still alive, I would still be running wit and for him, but since he's not; you're tha next best thing."

"Why didn't you just run with Ray-Ray like everybody else?"

"I don't like that Mafucka; never did."

"Ray-Ray will get what's coming to him."

Cam came out and posted up, "Mr. Willy you can fall back for a few hours, I'll take over."

"A'ight, I got a few errands to run anyway." For the next few hours it was non-stop money flowing.

"Cam take this ride wit me to tha crib to put this money up and grab some more work."

"I can't believe we ran through all that work; I better call Unc." I felt bad taking that 4½ but I wasn't about to let 4,500 get away."

The next day in school, I hollered at Titus.

"Damn, you want a stack an ounce?"

"I don't want Shit, my uncle does and he's gonna bet it's better than anything you can get ya hands on."

"When can I get it?"

"Whenever you want it?"

"After school."

"I can do even better if you got tha money on you I can it by lunch time."

"I'll meet you back here at lunch."

"Cool Titus, don't say nothing to Naf about this cause he'll tell my uncle and he doesn't deal wit kids."

"I'm not going to say Shit."

"Well, we can keep doing biz-ness."

"A'ight, we better get to class."

"See you lunch time and keep this between us."

"Naf talkin' bout I ain't cut out for hustling, yeah right."

"Nice to see you could join us."

"I was in tha restroom."

Titus walked in and handed the teacher a late pass. I looked at him and then winked to let him know that was smart thinking.

After class I walked up to Kamil, "Hey Cam what's good?"

"You tell me."

"I can't call it."

"Can I give you my number?"

"Sure, if you want to."

"Are you gonna use it?"

"Yeah, I wouldn't take it if I wasn't." I read my number off to her which she stored in her I-phone.

"Why do you want me to have ya number Cam, huh?"

"Look Kamil, let's cut tha Bullshit, I be seeing you checking me out."

"Ha! Ha! Ha! Boy you swear you got game, how you know I was checking you out if you ain't doing tha same?"

"I never said I wasn't."

"And neither did I, but somebody had to be tha one to initiate it."

"I know, that's why I told Shelly to tell you I liked you."

"Shelly ain't tell me nothing."

Shelly and Shalil came over with their lunch.

"We got you pizza and fries."

"Thanks," I said knowing they were talking to Kamil.

"Boy, you better back up."

"I know and why you over here talkin' to my sister?"

"I didn't know it was a crime to talk to my future girlfriend." Kamil started blushing.

"Cam beat it."

"Mil you better let them know we bout to be a couple." Mil couldn't stop smiling.

"I'll see you later, but if I don't, make sure you use that," I said pointing to her phone."

"I will."

I could hear them asking her questions. I slipped out without Naf seeing me so I could meet with Titus.

"Damn, I was beginning to think you changed ya mind."

"Nah, I had to go meet my uncle to pick it up."

"Wheew…This that Shit, right here."

"You probably could put something on it if you want to."

"Nah, this straight oils; they gonna love this Shit. If it's as good as it looks, I'll definitely be doing biz-ness."

"Here's my number, just hit me up tha day before so I can bring it to school."

"No problem." Naf was coming out of the cafeteria as I was going in.

"Where you was at?"

"My stomach was bubbling so I had to go."

While I was, in Math class my phone kept going off. When I finally looked at it I seen it was Mr. Willy. It had to be urgent since he knew I was in school.

"Ms. Hill, may I be excused to use the lavatory?"

"Make sure you take tha hall pass."

"What's up Mr. Willy?"

"Sorry to bother you in school, but we got a problem."

"What kind of problem?"

"Tha boy Sticky."

"I'm listening."

"He hit us for 3 ounces."

"Are you sure it was him?

"That fiend Mary said she saw him"

"A'ight, I'll be around in about an hour."

"Do you have enough to hold you down til then'?"

"Yeah."

"Imma have to make an example out of him, he done robbed tha wrong Mafucka this time." Shelly could sense something was wrong because she asked if everything was OK.

As soon as the bell rang I was out, I didn't even wait for Cam.

"Damn nigga wait up, what's going on?"

"That Mafucka Sticky got us for 3 onions."

"Imma finally get to use my pistol."

"Slow down, we need to be sure it was him first."

"What ever Nigga, it was him."

The block was jumping; cars and people were coming from every direction to buy crack.

"You a'ight out her Mr. Willy?"

"Well, since you asked, I could use a little help out here when you guys are in school or in tha crib for tha night."

"Did you have somebody in mind?"

"I was talking to tha young boy Kenny."

"Kenny from 23rd?"

"Yeah."

"I thought he was Fuckin' wit Ray-Ray?"

"He was but he said Ray-Ray played him."

"Figures."

"You know he use to be ya dad's Young Boy."

"Call him up and tell him to come through."

"Actually, he's on his way as we speak."

"Keep him around, I'll be back in 30 minutes."

"Gotta do ya homework first, I respect that Young Buck."

Cam already did his homework in class so he stayed outside.

"Hey Mr. Willy, where does Sticky live, do you know?"

"All I know is he has a baby mom that lives on the eastside."

"Where at on tha eastside?"

"Somewhere between 10th and 11th & Bennett." I didn't care what Nafee was talking about, Sticky has to go.

Up in The Studio Getting Blowed... This must be the realest Shit I ever wrote. Kenny pulled up bumpin' that 2 Pac in his .8 Wagon.

"Yo what up Willy?"

"You know what it is."

"So where is ya peeps at?"

"He had to handle something, he should be back in 30 minutes."

"My bag for taking so long, but I was knocking my young jawn off when you called; you know how that goes."

"Let me tell you right off tha bat, if he tells you to be somewhere at a certain time then you better be on time, not a minute later. Now, hold me down while I get this money."

"Yall got it jumping around here now, Shit I remember a few months back it was like a ghost town around this Mafucka."

"I know, but that was before my young buck came through; now it's like ants at a picnic."

"Aye Willy, I don't know what yall doing to this coke, but Man, Oh Man, it's tha best."

"I told you that."

"I done came all tha way from New Castle just to get this, so hook me up for my buck fifty."

"You gon' get what ya doe paid for. You know that Shack?"

"I know, but can you blame a brother for trying?"

"I'll do you a favor and hook you up only on one condition."

"What's that?"

"Turn all ya people's on."

"I was going to do that anyway; they got bullshit out my way."

"Just make sure you do," Mr. Willy said handing him his drugs.

"I want in on this thing yall got going on."

"Why you got them kids trappin?" Mr. Willy turned around to see what Kenny was talking about.

"Ha! Ha! Ha!"

"What's so funny?"

"Come on, Young Buck I want you to meet Kenny. Kenny this is Nafee," Kenny's whole facial expression changed.

"This is who you work for?"

"Yeah, ain't that something?"

"You look familiar. Do I know you from somewhere?"

"You use to run for his dad."

"Oh Shit, Samad!"

"Yup that's his pops."

"How old are you now?"

"12."

"And you got this Shit poppin' round here; like father like son."

"Mr. Willy tells me you wanna get down wit us."

"I'm trying to get a dollar, ever since ya dad died Shit has been Fucked up."

"What is up wit you and Ray-Ray?"

"Fuck Ray-Ray!"

Before I got the chance to ask he explained the story.

"Ray-Ray knew I was a good earner so when he killed ya dad, he came to me wit a biz-ness deal. At first it was sweet until Jimmy got in his ear. Then he jacked up tha number and tha work wasn't even that good."

"You should've just did ya own thing."

"I didn't have another plug."

"If you don't mind me asking, why you not Fuckin' wit him now?"

"Long story short, he cut me off and I've been trying to find a good plug ever since."

"Check this out, if you want to get down, this is how I do it. I'll front you an ounce for 1200; reason being I have tha best product in tha city."

"An ounce can take a half and still be good, but why do that when you can leave it as is and dump it much faster."

"I know Mr. Willy wanted you to help him but I believe wit this product ya block can be jumpin' just like this one."

"I have 5500 to come to tha table wit."

"That'll get you 5½ plus I'll front you 3½."

"Damn right, that's what's up; we gonna run this town in no time."

"Let me make one thing clear; Don't Fuck Me Over!"

"That was tha first thing ya dad said to me when I joined tha team."

"I'll be right back."

"He's another Samad, he didn't even know if he could trust me; he just put me on."

"I know that's why I have so much respect for him."

The next few months Money had more the tripled wit the help of Kenny.

"We need to tally up this money and call Uncle Kev."

"Whew, we getting this paper Baby; two hundred and thirty-one grand."

"Nafee, I think we should start selling weight."

"Nah, we doing just fine doing it like this."

"Fuck that Shit Naf!"

"Fuck what Cam?"

"We can make a lot more money selling weight."

"We don't need our names ringing like that. Our names already buzzing."

"No, they not. Well, let's step it up and grab 9 birds this time."

"Nah, we gon' grab tha same 2 birds we been grabbing."

"I'm tired of this nickel and dime Shit, I wanna blow."

"We are, just quietly Cam; trust me on this."

"How much work we got left?"

"5½," I said lying because I already took 4½ that I was selling to Titus tomorrow.

"You sure? I thought it was 10?"

"You wanna count it?"

"Nah, if you said it's 5½ than that's what it is."

"Well, Imma call Uncle Kev."

"A'ight, I need to walk to tha store for a Dutch, I'll be right back."

"Uncle Kev, what tha deal is?"

"I can't call it; what's good wit you?"

"I need tha same thing."

"Can you hold off til tha morning?"

"Nah, I only got 5½ left."

"I told you not to wait til you get down to tha bottom."

"I thought I had 10 left, but Cam said its 5½."

"Nephew, you need to get ya math right; you been miscounting a lot lately."

"Unc I also got a dilemma."

"Talk to me Naf."

"Cam wants to buy more and push weight."

"What do you want to do Naf?"

"Continue to do as I'm doing."

"Problem fixed."

"Yeah, but I don't want Cam to be mad."

"Naf, can I be completely honest wit you for a sec?"

"Of course."

"I love Cam like a nephew but you're doing all tha work while he's reaping tha benefits, so tha decision is yours. And I know that you can grab more than you are, but you choose not to; ya dad use to do tha same Shit, so you hustle at ya pace."

"Thanks Unc, I needed to hear that."

"Pete will be down in 45 minutes."

I have a funny feeling this is going to destroy their relationship later down the line.

CHAPTER 9

Finally

"Damn, I can never catch this Mafucka."

Just as I was about to pull off when I saw a light come on upstairs. For the last few months I been waiting for this nigga to show his face and I think tonight he will. I looked up in the window just in time to see him closing the blinds. I pulled around the corner so no one would see me jump into my car when I was done. Shit a few seconds later, and I would have let him get away.

"Excuse me, Sir."

"Excuse me," I said tapping on the driver side window.

"What's up kid?"

"Do you have some spare change?"

"Shouldn't you be in tha bed getting some sleep for school tomorrow?"

"I don't go to school," I said looking around to make sure nobody was watching and also looking to see if his gun was in arms reach. When I was sure it wasn't, I casually put my hand in my hoody to retrieve my pistol.

"Here Youngin' take this dollar."

"I'll take tha dollar but I want you to take this…"

(BOOM, BOOM, BOOM, BOOM) All four shots hit him in the face.

I casually walked back to my car so not to draw attention to myself.

CHAPTER 10

Divided

After school, we went straight to the block like always.

"What up Young Buck?"

"Same Shit different smell."

"Is this ya work?" he asked handing me the paper.

MAN SHOT EXECUTION STYLE WHILE IN CAR

"You got jokes."

"Read it."

I read the article, when it got to the name all I could say was, "Oh Shit!" I passed the paper back, "nah, that wasn't my work."

Cam read the article then said, "Fuck! Somebody beat me to it."

We both just looked at Cam but said nothing. I couldn't put my finger on it, but there was something different about Cam.

"My Man showed me how to hop that train the N.Y.C., how to stretch that cane make 5 outta 3."

"Hello."

"Naf, I'm ready for you."

"A'ight, give me about 30 minutes."

"Cool get me 9 this time."

"Gotcha!"

"Yo, I need to handle something, I'll be back."

"Imma stay here and hold Willy down."

"You sure? I'm bout' to holla at Kenny."

"Nah, go ahead."

"He'll sell Kenny weight, but nobody else."

"There's a reason for everything Young Buck."

"Cam!"

"Huh?"

"I told you my name is Cam, don't call me no Fuckin Young Buck; this my last time telling you," I said adjusting my pistol to let him know I wasn't playing."

"A'ight, a'ight, no need to get hostile."

I made a mental note to talk to Naf about Cam.

"Naf."

"Sup Kenny."

"I'm here."

"I'm pulling in now." I handed him the bag with 18 ounces.

"10.8."

"I know, but I got some folk from Maryland that's willing to pay top dollar."

"You could charge them up to 1,400 an ounce."

"How much would they be copping?"

"At least a half every two weeks." I quickly did the math in my head.

"A'ight, I'll give you a hundred off every ounce they buy and everything goes through you; make them think it's your work."

"I'm already two steps ahead of you."

"Well, set it up."

"I was hoping you said that, they're on standby."

"Call them see what they want."

"Hold up," he said pulling out his phone and pushing a button.

Within a few seconds, he was talking.

"Hey, did you let ya peeps sample that?"

"Yeah, and they said it was tha best Shit ever."

"I told you it was tha best on tha east coast."

"That you did and if tha number is tha same I'll take a bird now."

"Oh, you want a bird now?"

"Yeah, you got it?"

"Yeah, I got it."

"Can I get it for 50 flat?"

"50 Grand?" I quickly shook my head yes.

"Sure, meet me at tha spot."

"A'ight, I'll hit you when I get close."

"I'll meet you back here in 30 minutes. Imma need to call Uncle Kev and grab some more."

When I got to the crib I got the brick, put it in a bag and put the other half brick up. Look at it I knew it was short so, I decided to weight it. 374 grams, 126 short so I called Uncle Kev.

"What up Naf?"

"Uncle Kev I need to ask you something, but I don't want you to take it as disrespect or tha wrong way."

"Speak ya piece Naf."

"Was that tha whole two bricks?"

"Of course, you don't think ya young boy dipped in it; do you?"

"Hell Nah!"

"Why, what's up?"

"I just sold a bird in a half and it's 126 grams short."

"You sure?"

"Yeah, I'm positive, but it's not tha first time it was off."

"How come you never said nothing?"

"I just thought maybe it was me, but this is tha first time I touched it."

"Let me check Shit on my end and I'll get back wit you."

"Don't worry about it, just let me get 5 more."

"Naf, in this biz-ness if ya Shit is coming up short you deal wit it or else it will keep coming up short. I'll hit you in one hour."

"A'ight."

"Aye Clips let me holla at you real quick."

"What up Kev?"

"Imma ask you this one time and don't Bullshit me. Have you been dippin' in tha work you been taking to my nephew?"

"Hell Nah!"

"I didn't think so, but I still had to ask. That means Cam has been hittin' him. I knew it was only a matter of time before this happen."

"I thought they were brothers?"

"They are, but one wants to sell weight and tha other doesn't. Let me call him back. Naf."

"Yeah, Unc."

"I'm on my way, we need to talk."

"A'ight, I'll be here; I just need to pick this paper up."

"Is Cam wit you?"

"Nah, he on tha block. Do you want to talk to him too?"

"Nah, I just need to holla at you."

An hour later, Uncle Kev was walking through the door. I was just putting the last 25 Grand in the bag.

"Here, go put this up; matter fact, weight it first."

"Uncle I trust you."

"Good, cause that's what I wanna talk to you about. Cam is tha one who has been stealing from you."

"Nah Unc; we split everything 50/50. He doesn't have no reason to steal."

"Naf, I know ya dad taught you well so you should be able to see through all tha Bullshit. Jealousy is a mafucka."

"Why would he be jealous, he has tha same thing I have."

"Yeah, but who's making all tha money? Ya dad always told me there's only one way to catch a mouse and that's to put cheese on tha trap. All I'm saying is jealousy will make anybody change." On that note, Uncle Kev walked out the door.

Was Cam really stealing from me or should I say us. There was only one way to find out.

"Where tha Hell did you go…China?"

"How you know," I said laughing.

"Nigga you left two hours ago."

"I didn't know I had to check wit you."

"You don't Mafucka," Cam said getting upset

"I was wit Kenny across town peeping how his set was."

"Man, that Nigga doing stupid numbers, he Damn near sold all that Shit in a few hours."

"Yeah right."

"Word, he did, I had to call Unc and grab two more."

"I need to make a run, I'll be back I a little bit."

Titus had been blowing my phone up, he needed another 4½ and couldn't wait until school tomorrow. Since he just grabbed two more, he won't notice; he never does. After this, I'll have 22 Grand of my own doe that I made and he said hustling wasn't my thing, yeah a'ight. Shit, if it wasn't for me he wouldn't have Shit. I started this, but who gets all the credit, Naf. After taking care of Titus I went back to the block.

The next day I went to the crib and Uncle Kev was right there was 4½ missing.

"Hello."

"Aye Cam, did you grab some work?"

"Nah, why what's up?"

"Some work is missing."

"You sure?"

"Yeah."

"You probably misplaced it."

"Yeah, your probably right."

I couldn't believe Cam was actually betraying me and trying to make me think I was dumb at the same time. From that moment, I knew what had to be done.

"Listen Cam, I was thinking, since you want to sell weight and I don't we might as well do our own thing."

"I was thinking tha same thing, so just give me my share of tha doe." I went and got him 150 Grand.

"How much is this?"

"150 Grand."

"That's all I get?"

"We both get tha same thing."

For the next few months, Cam was doing his own thing, but the coke was trash because he was stepping on it too much. So, because of that he wasn't really making any money.

"Cam what's up wit this work you been hitting me wit?"

"Ain't nothing up wit it."

"Yeah it is, this Shit is trash."

"Funny you tha only one who says that."

"I need my money back, I can't move this Shit."

"I don't do refunds."

"Well, you not getting paid for tha Shit you fronted me then!"

"Oh, you gon' pay me," Cam said pulling out his 45.

"So, you gonna shoot me now?"

"Yup." *(BOOM)*

"AAAAHH Shit!"

"Get my money or tha next shot won't be in tha leg."

"DROP YA WEAPON NOW!" I turned around to be confronted by a cop who just happen to be walking the beat.

"PUT THA GUN DOWN SLOWLY!"

"Fuck!" I wanted to run, but I didn't want to get shot or even killed.

The sirens in the distance were getting closer. Finally, I put my gun down and got on my knee's as the cop told me to do. Next thing I knew, the cops were rushing me.

"YOU HAVE THE RIGHT TO REMAIN SILENT, ANYTHING YOU SAY CAN AND WILL BE USED AGAINST YOU!"

Everything after that just sounded like Charlie Browns Teacher Blah, Blah, Blah. All I could think about on the ride to the police station was spending the next 10 years' behind bars.

"Put him in Interview Room 3."

"We have to print him and log him in first."

"Can I call my mom?"

"What's the number, I'll have one of my men notify her."

"287-2424."

After I was finger printed, I was put in an Interview Room.

"Before you start, I'm not talking to anyone wit out my lawyer present."

"Kid you were caught by a police officer, so a lawyer is not going to help you outta this one. Hey Mike, put him in Juvy 4. Did anybody get hold of his mother?"

"I'm calling now Sarg."

"Hello."

"Yes, this is Detective Owens, can I speak to Ms. White please?"

"This is her."

"We have your son in custody."

"My son for what?"

"Attempted murder."

"Attempted murder? Detective there must be some mistake!"

"I'm afraid not, is your son Camron White?"

"Yes."

"Then there is no mistake."

"I'm on my way." Before I could say anything else the line went dead.

"Cookie, Oh My God Cookie!"

"Calm down Jonda what's tha matter?"

"Cam's at tha police station."

"For what?"

"Tha detective said attempted murder."

"Jonda, April Fools isn't til next week."

"I'm not playing, my Baby is locked up."

"Are you home?"

"Yes."

"I'm on my way. Naf…Nafee!!!"

"Yes Mom."

"Get ya shoes on and come on."

"Where we going?"

"Don't question me just do what I said!"

I didn't know what was going on, but I knew it wasn't good. Ms. Jonda was outside waiting when we pulled up.

"Did they say what happened?"

"No, he just said Cam was being charged wit attempted murder." I know I didn't just hear her say what I thought she said.

"Nafee, do you know what happened?"

"No, I've been in tha crib doing my book report and I thought Cam was doing the same."

"I'm Camron White's mother."

"Ms. White, Detective Owens is expecting you. One minute while I call him up front. Detective Owens, Ms. White is here to see you. You can have a seat, he'll be right up." Five minutes later, a tall medium built guy came out.

"Ms. White."

"Yes."

"I'm Detective Owens," he said with his hand extended.

"Who did my son try to kill?"

"If you will follow me, this way we can talk in private."

"A'ight but this is my sister and nephew, they'll be joining us."

"That's fine with me." We went up some stairs to a small office in the back.

"Excuse me while I get another chair."

"That's OK. I'm cool."

"Well, Ms. White, one of our patrol officers was walking his beat when he observed your son shooting Titus McMann in the leg."

"TITUS!" I yelled out.

"Do you know him?"

"Yeah, he goes to school wit us."

"Do you know of any problems they had?"

"Nah."

"Ms. White, do you know where your son could have gotten the gun from?"

"No, my son is a good kid, he wouldn't have done this for no reason. This Titus kid had to do something to him," my mom added, "wait a minute Nafee, isn't that tha boy you got into a fight wit last year?"

"Yes, be we've spoken since then."

"Detective, if he only shot him in tha leg, why is he charged wit attempted murder?"

"Anytime somebody is shot below the waist and lives, that's what it is."

"No Detective, actually, if he lives it will drop to 1st Degree Assault and tha other charges that go along with it."

"You seem to know a lot about the law Ms. Jackson."

My mom said, "I have 2 years' of law under by belt. Are they gonna give my son bail?"

"I doubt it, he'll probably go to the Detention Center while he waits for trial."

"I would like to see him if it's possible."

"I'm afraid that won't be."

"Could you give him a message?"

"That I can do."

"Let him know I'll be to see him as soon as they let me and I love him." I could tell this was tearing her up; I would never want to put my mom through what Aunt Jonda is going through right now.

"There are a few good lawyers I know that you could call."

"I just need tha best one."

"Then you need to call Joe Hurley; he's one of the best. Give me your phone so I can store his number in it."

"Cookie, thank you so much for being here."

"You know you don't have to thank me, you would do tha same if it were me."

"I'll call you tomorrow after I talk to tha lawyer."

"OK, if you need me or need to talk don't hesitate to call me." They gave each other a sisterly hug before we pulled off.

"Nafee you don't know what happened?"

"No Mom, truth be told me and Cam haven't been spending much time together lately."

"Funny you mentioned that, I've been meaning to ask you about that."

"He thinks that I'm suppose to agree wit everything he says or does and I don't."

"Mom we are getting older so a lot of tha stuff I use to do or like, I'm outgrowing it."

"Baby, I understand, I just don't want you out in tha streets runnin' crazy."

"You don't have to worry about that."

The next few weeks were hectic; I saw Titus in school and found out what had happened.

"Naf, I don't want to go to court, but my mom is forcing me."

"How long has Cam been selling you weight?"

"Even since that day we talked, he said that ya uncle was giving it to him." Now it was all adding up and making sense. I couldn't believe Cam had been taking Shit all that time.

"Listen Titus, they caught him red-handed wit tha gun so it doesn't matter if you go or not, but I will give you 5 stacks not to show."

"How can I refuse that."

"I'll give yo half now and tha other half when it's done."

"No more needs to be said and does ya uncle still have that fire?"

"Yup."

"Hook a Nigga up then."

"Give me ya number and I'll hit you up in a few days." I had a visit to see Cam with Aunt Jonda after school. I couldn't wait to talk to him.

"Hey Naf, how is Cam doing?"

"He cool."

"I wrote him, but he never responded back."

"He has a lot on his plate right now, I'll let him know you asked about him when I visit today."

"Did you finish ya Science project yet?"

"Nah."

"You better get a move on it, it's due next Friday."

"I know, why don't you come over tomorrow and help me finish it."

"OK." Shelly was really on me, but I wasn't giving her any play. Let's just say I've been playing hard to get.

"Naf, come on I don't wanna be late." We arrived at the Detention Center as they were changing shifts. Cam was already in the Visiting

Room when we got in there. I could tell he was working out.

"What up Stranger?"

"I can't call it, how they treating you in this piece?"

"Like I'm a Ward of tha State. Mom did you bring me those sneakers?"

"Oh Shit, I left 'em in tha car, I'll be right back."

I didn't even wait for her to get out the room before I started with my questions.

"So why did you shoot Titus?"

"He was talkin' Shit in class."

"Cam, I thought we were better than that."

"We are."

"Then cut tha Bullshit! I know you shot him because he didn't want to sell that trash you gave him."

"Well, if you knew why tha Fuck did you ask me?"

"I wanted to see if you were going to lie or not. Not that it matters, but he's not going to court."

"I'm not taking it to trial, I'm going to take tha plea of 6 years."

"I'll hold you down, you know that." I was about to say something smart when my mom came back with my LeBron's.

"Thanks Mom, what would I do wit out you?"

"Did he tell you he was taking tha plea deal they offered him?"

"He just told me." We talked for the rest of the visit; well, actually they talked and I listened.

"VISITS OVER!" the guard called out.

"Put my number on ya phone list and hit me up."

I gave him a hug and headed out so he and Aunt Jonda could say their goodbye's.

Once we were back in the car Aunt Jonda let me know that Cam would probably be sentenced in 2 to 3 weeks depending on the lawyer's schedule.

"Naf, he said to tell you that he loves you like a brother. No matter what you might think of him."

CHAPTER 11

Guilty Plea

"Mr. White, you signed this plea on your own free will?"

"Yes."

"Then I will accept this plea bargain and sentence you to 6 years' with 6 months of probation to follow."

"Your Honor if I may."

"Go head counsel."

"My client is twelve, he'll be eighteen when he is released. With all due respect, I don't think it's fair for him to have to start his adult life in the system."

"Mr. Hurley, you make a good point. So, I'll disregard the probation. Mr. White I'm going to stipulate that you get your diploma while incarcerated."

"Yes Sir."

"That's it…Next Case!" I turned to face my mom who had tears in her eyes as did Aunt Cookie.

"I love yall."

"We love you too."

CHAPTER 12

Mad at the World

It seemed as if high school came and went; I was actually graduating next week. My mom and Aunt Jonda went to Cam's graduation last week, he was now in Howard R. Young (HRYC) on this poo called Y-cop for Juveniles who were charged as adults. Me and Shelly have been messing around for about a year now.

"Naf, Mil showed me this picture Cam sent her. He's been hitting tha weights I see."

"Yeah, all he got is time; he should be in shape."

"Yall still not talking?"

"Shelly, for tha last 4 years' I've been holding him down and he doesn't appreciated Shit."

"Baby, you gotta understand, he's locked up."

"I didn't put him there. He did that to himself."

"Yeah, but you still have to understand, nobody wants to be caged in like a wild animal."

"I have a visit to see him next Wednesday so I can get some Shit off my chest."

I finally got my driver's license and my mom treated me to a nice Cadillac Escalade. I put the 26's on it, but she thought Uncle Kev brought them along with the 10,000-sound system.

"Shelly I'll call you later, I need to make a few runs."

"I'll probably be at ya house; my mom and Ms. Cookie are helping me pick out a prom dress."

"Well, I don't get off work til 6 o'clock."

Shelly and my mom thought I was working at Uncle Kev's detail shop, but what they didn't know was that we were partners. I talked Uncle Kev into going in with me so I could clean my money up. The last 4 years' have been very good for me to say the least. I've monopolized most of the city without being known or in the spotlight.

"What up Boss?"

"I told you about that boss Shit Nigga!"

"There you go getting all sentimental on a Mafucka."

"Nah, I just don't like that boss Shit."

"Hey Man you tha boss."

"Did you hear about tha boy Nate?"

"Which Nate?"

"Nate that lives on Rodney."

"Nah, what happen?"

"He was shot 10 times."

"Did he die?"

"Nah, but he's in critical condition."

"I told him to stop being Flamboyant. Trap some Niggaz don't know how to bubble and stay low."

"like you Huh?"

"I don't know what you talkin' bout."

"Naf, I been in tha game too long not to see a smart hustler."

"Trap, how old are you?"

"23."

"And how long you been hustling?"

"8 years."

"Not to be in ya biz-ness, but how much you coppin?"

"Half brick."

"Why you only doing a half, if you been in tha game 8 years."

"That is a question I often ask myself."

"Who you dealing wit?"

"Ray-Ray."

"That's tha answer right there."

"I tried to holla at Kev, but he don't do biz-ness down here no more since my old head Samad was killed. Now when he was alive may he Rest in Peace, everybody ate and tha prices was affordable."

"How come Ray-Ray is charging so much and they say tha work ain't that good?"

"Because nobody will cross him since he killed Samad."

"Why?"

"Well, you probably not old enough to know, but Samad was a powerful man so for him to kill him spoke in volumes."

"You seem like you had a lot of respect for Samad."

"Had Nah, I still got respect for him. Tha only reason I deal wit Ray-Ray is because I don't have no other supplier. So, what other choice do I have, but to pay 25,200 for tha half."

"Trap I've liked you since you started working here last year, but seeing how much respect you have for my dad just sealed it."

Looking puzzled he said, "Huh?"

"Samad is my dad and I was old enough to know how much power he had, that's why I couldn't understand why nobody killed Ray-Ray."

"Me either, tha one time I tried, tha gun jammed so I took it as a sign it wasn't for me to do it."

"So, you was gonna ride for my pops?"

"Hell Yeah!"

"Come on back in my office so we can talk in private. I'm gonna save you 7200 and hit you wit tha best coke on tha east coast."

"I knew you was in tha game."

"Well, I'll hit you wit half brick for 18 Grand and I'll throw you a half, but I'll need 21.6 back since it's on consignment."

"No problem."

"Get wit me after work and this stays between us."

"Naf, I'm a real Nigga."

"I know or you wouldn't know I had weight."

"I know a lot of people that want weight and who are looking for tha change to cut Ray-Ray off."

"Cool, but I don't want to be involved. Everything goes through you, for all they know you tha man."

"Hold on Kenny and Willy." I just shook my head.

"We bout to get PAAAID and shut Ray-Ray DOWN WHEEEEW!" After Trap got off he called me and I hit him wit a brick.

"ALL 2:30 VISITS COME THIS WAY PLEASE."

Cam was already sitting in a booth when I got there. I could tell he was surprised to see me.

"I see you still working out."

"Yeah, that's all I can do in here."

"Did you get tha money and pictures I sent you?"

"Yeah, good looking out."

"I bought another 500 today so you should be good for another 5 months."

"That's what's up."

"But on some serious Shit, you need to show Aunt Jonda some respect."

"Naf, don't go there, my mom was suppose to do something and she didn't so."

"So, what? You refuse to call or see her?"

"You Mafuckin' right. If I tell her to do something, that's all it is."

"Even if it puts her in harm's way?"

"How is meeting a guard putting her in harm's way?"

"Do I really need to answer that?"

"You could've hit me and asked me to do what you wanted Aunt Jonda to do."

"Nigga for what? So, you could have something else to talk about?"

"Is that what you think that I do Shit to gloat because if you do your wrong."

"Naf, all ya life you always had to have tha spotlight."

"If it wasn't for me you never would've gotten into tha game and as soon as you did you took over."

"You didn't have to do Shit, but watch my back and I split everything

50/50 wit you despite tha fact you were stealing from us. Yeah, I know about all tha coke you took. If you would've listened to me then all that could've been prevented. Tha crazy thing is you did all that and don't have Shit to show for it so let me ask you. Was it worth it Cam?"

"I was only 12."

"And so was I."

"You Shit in tha same spot you was in 4 years' ago Naf."

"Cam I own a detail shop, I got Maryland on lock as well as 70% of tha city and nobody knows it's me so if you consider that in tha same spot then yeah, I am in tha same spot." The guard came to let us know the visit was over.

"Cam I'm still ya brother and I got ya back no matter what."

"How was ya visit Cam?"

I wasn't in the mood for conversation so I just got in my rack. Naf was eating like a fat chick at a buffet. I know I should be happy for him, but I wasn't. All I could think about was taking everything he had. I laid my head on my pillow and before I knew it I was out.

"Cam, Cam."

"Yo."

"Food cart here."

"I ain't eating, you can have mines Nigga. You know I don't want that fish."

"You A'ight? You seemed mad after ya visit?"

"I'm good, my brother know how to get to me."

"Man, my Damn brother do tha same Shit."

"You cooking tonight?"

"Nah Nigga, I cooked last night."

"I'm making a Grand."

"I don't care as long as you make two."

Scrap has been my cell mate for two months, he was sentenced to 2 years' for Assault 2nd.

MAIL CALL: WHITE, PERKINS…

"These tha flicks I was waiting for," Scrap said wit a big smile.

I looked at the name on my envelope and smiled.

"Must be wifey."

"I don't have no wifey."

"What ever Nigga."

"LOCK IN FOR CLEAN UP!"

As soon as I got in the room I opened my mail.

"Damn Kamil lookin' good as Shit."

I read the letter.

Dear Cam,

    How you doing in there? I finally got a recent picture of myself so I decided to send it. I'm glad you finally started writing me, I've been missing you a lot. My mom says that it's OK for me to visit so ask ya mom if she could put me on tha list to come see you. Here's my number so she can call and you too. Well I don't have much

<u>to say in this letter.</u>

Love,

Kamil Ya#1 Fav

<u>P.S. Shelly and Nafee Hot and Heavy (LOL)</u>

As soon as I read that my attitude came back.

"Here's my brother right here."

"Oh Shit!"

"What's up?"

"Ray-Ray ya brother?"

"Yeah, you know him?"

"Who don't know Ray-Ray; he eatin' all crazy, no wonder ya books stay stacked."

"This my peeps right here," I said handing him the picture of Kamil.

"Daaaamn Nigga, you better wife her before somebody else get her. She bad as a Mafucka."

"She's a twin too."

"You mean to tell me there's another one of her?"

"Yeah."

"Hook a brother up."

"I'll see what I can do for you."

"Bet my Nigga."

"They need to hurry up I gotta use tha phone."

CHAPTER 13

Prom Night

"Thanks Uncle Kev for letting me use ya Maybach."

"Naf, it's ya prom night you gotta give 'em something to talk about."

"I'm sure they'll be talkin' bout this, we gonna have 'em hatin' for real."

Shelly decided to wear pink & cream. She had a Vera Wang original that my mom, Ms. Porsha and she put together; while I had a cream Armani Suit with a pink Armani Shirt and shoes to match. After I put her corsage on they took pictures.

"We gonna be late Mom."

"Boy shut up and put ya glasses on."

"Look at my Baby."

"Mom don't start please."

"Naf here's a little graduation present I got for you."

When I opened the box all I could say was, "Oh Shit!" My mom smacked me in the back of my head.

"Boy you better watch ya mouth."

"Sorry Mom." It was a Cartier Watch with my initials in diamonds across the face. My mom looked at Uncle Kev and then smiled.

"If ya dad was alive he would be proud right now."

Forty-five minutes later, we were pulling up in front of the Hotel DuPont in Uncle Kev's white on white Maybach, sitting on deuces deuces dumpin' Rick Ross's Here I Am. All eyes were definitely on us. Kamil and Shalil were standing out front waiting on us to get out.

"I knew that had to be yall pulling up in that Hot Ass whip. Look at yall, Naf we have to take some pictures for Cam, I told him I would send him some pictures."

"Mil & Lil yall look real nice."

"Thank you Naf."

"I wish Cam could be here."

"Me too," I said.

"I have a visit to see him next week."

"I know, Aunt Jonda told me."

"She is so nice."

"Come on let's get this party started."

"I heard that." We danced our butts off all night.

CAN WE HAVE EVERYBODY'S ATTENTION PLEASE. IT'S TIME TO ANNOUNCE THIS YEARS' KING AND QUEEN. THIS YEARS' KING IS NAFEE JACKSON AND QUEEN IS SHELLY BROWN. EVERYBODY WAS HOLLERING LIKE CRAZY.

When the prom was over we all decided to hit the Waffle House to get some grub. Since Mil & Lil's mom dropped them off, they rode with us.

"I can't believe yall didn't come wit no date tha way Niggaz be all on yall."

"I can't speak for Lil, but my man is on lock down so that's why I came by myself."

"Naf ou know them Niggaz only want one thing and my momma didn't raise no fool."

"I heard that," said Shelly dapping her.

"So, you and Cam really serious huh?"

"Yeah, she finally wore him down," said Lil. *(Ha! Ha! Ha!)* We all had to laugh at that, even Mil.

"What ever, you just mad."

"Never would I be mad at my sistah for having a man."

"We aren't tha only ones hungry," Shelly said referring to all the cars.

I parked right in front so I could keep an eye on Uncle Kev's car.

"Nice whip Naf."

"Thanks, but it's my uncle's."

"Figured that, you can't afford no Shit like that I'll bring by Benz by tha shop so you can clean it." *(Ha! Ha! Ha!)* Everybody laughed.

I took my suit jacket off and put it in the car.

"Come on Naf, don't feed into it."

"I'm not."

"Nice watch, I seen tha same one in tha Chinese store window." *(Ha! Ha! Ha!)*

"My watch cost just as much as that outdated Benz you drive."

"OOOOh Daaaamn!"

"Come on yall." The waiter showed us to our table.

"That is a nice watch Naf."

"Thanks Mil."

"Did it really cost as much as his car?" Lil asked.

"He don't know, his uncle got it for him for graduation."

"Well, it sure looks like it cost a lot wit all these diamonds in it." We talked while we waited for out food.

"Oh God, here they come again!"

I turned to see Sharky and his boys coming towards us with some bald White man. Sharky was the type dude who always wanted the spotlight and to show off. I knew he wouldn't last long in the game.

"Naf this is my jeweler, I told him about ya watch and he wanted to see it for himself." Now everybody had gathered around.

"Sharky, I don't got to prove nothing to you or anybody else."

"I told yall that Shit was fake. Now pay me my money."

"Damn Naf, you just cost me 500."

"Only because I don't want to see you lose ya money." I put my wrist up so he could see it, I could tell by his face it was worth a few ones.

"I heard somebody say what's it worth?"

"Sharky I have to be honest those are real diamonds; I would have to say this watch cost at least 25."

"My charm cost 2500."

"No, No 25 Grand probably more."

"Shit! Give me my money Sharky."

"Man, I got you."

"Nah nigga pay me."

"Mafucka you act like you not gonna get ya money," he said pulling out a wad of bills.

After he peeled out five C-notes, he put one on the table and said, "This meal is on me."

"We can pay for our own food," said Shelly.

"I'm sure you can, but tonight it's on me." The waiter came with our food.

"This is a tip for you," I said sliding him the C-note.

"Wow, thank you Young Man."

"Thank him," I said pointing to Sharky.

"Thank you, Sir."

"What ever," he said walking off.

We dropped Mil & Lil off then headed to the Marriot. Uncle Kev had gotten me a room. He said he'd done the same thing for my mom and dad after their prom. I couldn't help but smile when I thought about the safe sex speech my mom and Ms. Porsha gave us.

"Now we know that you tow are in love and prom night will probably be tha night you both lose your virginity so we got you these." Me and Shelly busted out laughing.

"What's so funny?"

"This isn't our first time and yes we use condoms." The look on their faces was priceless.

"Cookie here we are all nervous to have this conversation and they already doing tha do."

"Well, that explains why ya Ass is sprouting."

"What you thinking about Naf?"

Our moms and their sex speech.

"Now that was funny."

"No what was funny was tha look on their faces when you told them we were already having sex."

Shelly went into the bathroom to shower, 20 minutes later, she emerged with this black Victoria Secret Teddy on looking beautiful.

"I'll be back, let me jump in tha shower."

I heard Alicia Keys singing about *'Sleeping with a Broken Heart'* while I was in the shower. I stepped out the shower to be greeted by the smell of cinnamon mixed with vanilla. I wrapped my towel around my waist and walked out.

"Umm Papi, you look good," Shelly said in her cutest Spanish accent.

"Gracias," I replied.

I still trained every day so my body was intact. That night was the first time in a year that we made love and boy was it something special.

CHAPTER 14

Warned

Another year had flown by and everything was looking good. The detail shop was doing extremely well. Everybody who was anybody brought their car to have it done up. The coke game was doing well despite taking a few losses at the hands of Ray-Ray. Uncle Kev let me buy out his 10% of the shop, but he told my mom he sold me the shop for 5 Grand. Even though she wanted me to go to college she was still happy for me. I let her know when I turned 18, I was getting my own place. I could tell she wasn't very happy about it, but she understood I was getting older and needed my privacy.

"Jimmy I wanna know who this Mafucka is that's supplying my town with this good coke."

"Ray-Ray we been trying to figure that out for tha past year and still haven't come up wit Shit."

"This Mafucka is cutting into my biz-ness."

"I need to get my hands on some of this Shit."

"I'm two steps ahead of you on that, Jake is on his way now wit an ounce."

(KNOCK, KNOCK)

"Who is it?"

"Jake."

"Come on in."

"What up Jimmy, Ray-Ray?"

"What tha biz is Jake?"

"Same Shit, I got that work you wanted."

"Let me see it."

"This look like that Shit my uncle be having. Hand me my phone off tha table Jimmy." I called my mom to get Kev's number.

"Yall finally bout to make up after all these years."

"I doubt that Mom, I just need to holla at him for a sec."

"I need to call you back, let me find out if he wants you to have his number or not."

"Fuck that Mafucka!"

"Boy, you better watch ya mouth when you talkin' to me."

"My fault Mom, just call and hit me back."

"Hey Sis, is everything a'ight?"

"Ya nephew just called me wanting ya number."

"Did he say for what?"

"No."

"Get a pen and give him this number."

"Hold on while I get a pen."

"OK what's tha number?"

"215.444.5432."

"Do I need to keep this for myself?"

"No, you have tha numbers you need."

"A'ight."

"How are you feeling?"

"You know some days are better than others."

"Do you need anything?"

"No."

"You sure?"

"Kevin, you do enough just paying my medical bills every month and I know that was you who put that money into my account."

"What money?"

"Kevin besides me your tha only one who knows my account number."

"Busted."

"I'll be down this weekend, let's do lunch."

"Sounds good to me, love ya."

"Love ya more, Big Sis."

"Damn, it don't take that long to get a Fuckin' number. Bout' time Hello."

"215.444.5432."

"Hold up Mom, let me store it; now repeat tha number."

"215.444.8432."

"Thanks, talk to you later."

"I need you to drop me off a few dollars so I can pay for my medicine."

"I thought your insurance covers it?"

"If it did, would I be asking you for money?"

"Why didn't you ask ya brother?"

"Because I asked you and don't question me."

"I'll drop it off later."

As soon as I hung up I dialed the number that she had just given me. After 4 rings, somebody answered.

"Yo."

"What up Kev?"

"I'm listening."

"How you been Unc?"

"Cut tha small talk. What you want?"

"Always to tha point, well there seems to be a lot of your product in my city."

"And?"

"You wouldn't happen to know anything about that, now would you?"

"I do a lot of biz-ness all over tha east coast so it wouldn't surprise me if it's floating around down there."

"Do you think you can keep ya Shit out my city?"

"Ha! Ha! I don't have no control over that."

"Listen here! If you don't everybody that's pushin' it will be dealt wit accordingly."

"Nah, let me tell you something before you start making treats you better know this is tha major not tha minor leagues you playing in so if you come, you better come correct."

"Mafucka I'm not afraid of you or anybody else, you understand that you bleed just like me!"

"You need to understand tha only reason you're still alive is because of my sister. If it wasn't for her being sick, you would be a memory Raymond." The phone went dead.

"Who tha Fuck does that Bitch Nigga think he is talkin' to me like that! We need to hit tha streets hard and find out who's buying this Shit from

him and flooding my city wit it. And if they don't talk, we'll send a message loud and clear."

I knew it was only a matter of time before this happened. Since I was having lunch with my sister in two days I would talk to Nafee face to face, but until then I called to give him a heads up.

"Where do you want to eat lunch Sis?"

"Let's go to Olive Garden I got a taste for some of that Shrimp Alfredo."

Me and my sister caught up on each other's lives over lunch.

"Kevin, your nephew is disrespectful and to tell you tha truth I'm so tired of him."

"What do you mean disrespectful?"

"His mouth and every time I ask him to do something he acts like I'm asking for a million dollars."

"Shy you're my Sis and you know I'll move mountains for you."

"I know you will."

"As long as I'm alive you don't have to ask him for Shit."

"It's just you live all tha way in Philly and I don't want you to keep runnin' back and forth for me when my son is right here."

"I need to have a talk wit Raymond."

"Kevin let me say this, I may have cancer, but I'm not dumb."

"I know that you and Samad were like brothers because he was like a brother to me."

"I heard rumors that Raymond was responsible for Samad's death."

"You can't always believe what you hear Sis."

"I didn't have to hear it to know it was true; your actions said it all."

"You use to love Raymond; Hell, you nicknamed him Ray-Ray, so for you to just disown him I knew he did it."

"Sis, you know I'd never lie to you."

"Kevin, I know, you don't have to say it and I am grateful."

"You know he threatened me today."

"I had no idea, that's why he wanted ya number."

"It's a'ight, I told him to stay in his lane."

"Shy, Raymond's gonna get himself in some Shit he can't get out of."

"Do you want me to talk to him?"

"For what? It's gonna go in one ear and out tha other."

"Kevin, I already prepared myself for that phone call."

"Shy, I will promise you that if something does happen, it won't be by my hands or my call."

"I know it won't because you would have done it by now." We finished lunch and then I drove her home.

"Kevin, I need to stop and pick up my weed." I looked at her like she lost her mind.

"Oh Boy, please they got me on this weed for my cancer," she said showing me her medication card.

"They probably giving you some Bullshit, you need some of this," I said pulling out my sandwich bag of sour diesel.

"That might be too much for me."

"If they telling you weed will cure your cancer, then this is what you want; trust me," I said passing her the sandwich bag.

"If you insist."

"Call me and let me know if you need some more."

"I will."

"Where do you have to pick up your prescription?"

"I don't need it now."

"Sis, you still need to pick it up so it won't look obvious."

"I guess you're right; I didn't think about that." Once I dropped her off I shot by the shop where I knew Nafee would be.

"What up Kev, what brings you down this way?"

"I was just having lunch wit my Sista and figured I'd drop by to check up on my nephew."

"Word."

"How is everything around here?"

"Man biz-ness is booming."

"That's what I like to hear. I see yall done added a game room."

"Yeah, Naf said it would give them something to do while they wait on their car."

"Damn, yall even got food."

"Yeah."

"No wonder biz-ness is booming; my nephew sure knows how to get that money."

"You ain't never lied about that," Trap said with a big smile.

Nafee told me he put Trap on, which I thought was a good idea since Trap knew how to get at a dollar.

"Uncle Kev, how long you been here and why you ain't hit me to let me know you was on ya way down?"

"I just got here and I told you I was having lunch wit my Sista today."

"Oh Shit! That's right."

"Love what you've done to tha place."

"Thanks."

"That's why I sold it to you, I knew you would make it evolve into a money machine."

"Let's go in tha back so we can talk."

"Hey Trap, do me a favor, have somebody detail my car."

"No problem, Kev Gotcha!"

"The reason I wanted to talk to you is because Ray-Ray called my phone saying that your product is interfering wit his biz-ness."

"Excuse my language Fuck his biz-ness!"

"He's talking about runnin' down on everybody who has tha product."

"He's gonna have to do a lot of runnin' down, I control 80% of tha city now."

"Wow, you are ya fathers' son, Naf, I told Ray-Ray that he might be out of his league."

"Unc Imma let my peoples know to handle their biz-ness if need be."

"I'm not trying to be in tha middle of a war."

"I've been on tha low for 4 years' now and I plan to keep it that way."

"I feel what you saying, but never let a Mafucka force ya hand."

"My dad use to tell me tha same thing."

"Naf, ya dad was a smart man."

"Uncle Kev I've always respected you and no matter what that will never change; I just hope that when it's all said and done…"

"You don't have to say another word, I knew tha day would come that you would want to revenge your father's death."

"So, you have no objections how I handle this?"

"Naf if it wasn't for my Sista, Ray-Ray would've been 6 feet under a long time ago."

"That's all I needed to hear; so, I would continue to take over all of Ray-Ray's biz-ness, and then he'll be dealt wit."

"Just make sure you put ya folks on point."

"That has already been taken care of."

"A'ight, I'll call you; I need to get back up top to take care of some biz-ness."

CHAPTER 15

Count Down

"Aye Scrap, it's almost over Baby!"

"6 months and we up outta here."

"Damn, I only been down 18 months and I'm ready so I know you ready after doing 6 mandy."

"I'm not going to lie, it seemed like forever, I'm just ready to roll."

"You wanna smoke this now or wait til after count time?"

"Nigga light that Shit up!"

"Say no more."

"Wheeew! This some good Shit!"

"I got my brother to send some sour diesel."

"I thought you wasn't Fuckin wit him like that?"

"Yo Wilks is coming around to count."

"Fuck 'em, he ain't gonna say Shit unless he smells it."

When Wilks came by he tapped on the window with a thumbs up.

"Nigga what you jumpin' for?"

"I thought he was coming in."

"Ha, Ha, you all high and paranoid."

"Man, you know Wilks be on his Bullshit."

"Who you think brought this Shit in?"

"Say word."

"Word."

"Oh Shit, I thought Adams hit you off." Adams was the 8-4, five-day officer who always hit Scrap off.

"We can blow all day long for this last 6 months."

"And you know it," I said dapping him.

"Shit, we gonna be so on, by tha time we look up they gonna by saying White, Perkins bag and baggage."

"You max out 2 weeks before me, all I want is for you to fall back until I get there."

"Cam, I already told you what it's hittin' for."

"Cool, let's go out here and take these Niggaz money on tha Dominoes table."

CHAPTER 16

Enough

"I'm not going to ask you again, where you get this work from?"

"I told you my peeps in Maryland."

"Nigga you lying!" *(BOOM)*

"Aaaagh Fuck!"

"Make this ya last time on my block; next time it's not going to be a leg shot. Let's go Jimmy."

"I still think we should've sent his Punk Ass to tha boneyard."

"All we doing is sending a message." The next few stops we came up empty.

"The word must have spread we were coming thru."

"Fuck it we'll come back through later."

"Oh Shit!"

"What's up?"

"I was suppose to drop some money off to my mom. Damn I forgot, let me call her."

"Hello," my mom said real groggy.

"Mom, I'm on my way wit that money."

"Don't bother my brother took care of it."

"Well…*(Click) I know she didn't hang up on me. I swear I wish she go ahead and kick tha bucket, I'm sick of her Shit!*"

"Damn Dog that's ya mom you don't mean that."

"Yes, I do; she thinks I'm suppose to jump when she say jump. I let Kev's Bitch Ass do that."

"Dog remember you only get one mom so, don't say something you might regret later."

"Nigga I been doin' this Shit by myself my whole life."

"We been doin' this Shit together for tha last 10 years."

"That's why I got a lot of love for you Nigga."

"I had to get me a few dipsticks so I could relax I was under a lot of stress tha city that I once had was slippin' away."

"Naf, I just got a call from Lou, he said J.R. was shot."

"How bad is he hurt?"

"It was only a leg shot, he'll make it."

"I don't need to ask who did it, I guess that's his way of trying to get my attention."

"Yup."

"Well, he got it I don't agree wit his methods."

"He's lost a lot of money over tha past year so he's feeling it."

"I was going to let him keep tha 20% he has, but now Fuck' em!"

"Get Creep and Lava to hit tha control."

"Gotcha!"

"Even since I put Trap on he's become my right hand, not only is he bout this paper, he also has no problem puttin' in work."

"Naf they're on their way to take care of that as we speak."

"Good."

"You know this Shit might get a little messy?"

"I'm well aware of it, take a ride wit me."

"Where we going? I'm on tha clock."

"I need to drop this weed and cell phone off for my brother."

"I thought he comes home in 6 months?"

"He does, but he wanted a cell phone."

"What is he gonna do when he get this paper?"

"Trap I don't even know, he was never tha money type, he was tha gun."

"I heard he was bout his biz-ness at tha age of 12."

"If you consider shooting somebody in tha leg about his biz-ness then yeah I guess he is."

"I wasn't talking about that."

"Well then, you lost me."

"Come on Naf, it's me; if you don't know by now you can trust me then you never will."

"I know I can trust you, but I have no idea what you're talking about."

"So, you didn't know he killed Sticky?"

"Nah, I had my suspicions though."

"My cousin said he saw tha whole thing." He went on to describe what his cousin said happened.

"Hold up while I holla at this dude."

"Naf what's up?"

"Same Shit Wilk."

"Did you get tha phone I told you to get?"

"Yeah and tell him to be easy wit it."

"He already knows tha deal."

"Here's an extra 500, don't spend it all in one place."

"Imma treat my young jawn to this Prada Hand Bag she wants."

"Don't let her burn a hole in ya pockets."

"I know that's right."

"Let me get outta here; I'll see you same time next week."

"A'ight, you be safe Naf."

"Always Wilks always."

"How you get hooked up wit him?"

"Cam sent him at me."

"It's amazing how a Mafucka can be in tha bing and still feel like he's on tha streets."

"Trap you know jail is like tha underworld."

"Yeah, they know about Shit before tha streets do."

"Oh Shit!"

"What's up?"

"I forgot I have to pick Shelly something up for her birthday."

"I thought it was this weekend?"

"It is, but I still have to get her something."

"Nigga you need to get her a car so you don't have to keep breaking ya neck every time your phone rings." *(Ha! Ha! Ha!)*

"Fuck you Trap!"

"Seriously though, we can hit tha auction and you can find something nice, cheap and reliable."

"What days do they have tha auction?"

He looked at his watch and said, "In 30 minutes."

"Let's go then."

"Pull over, let me drive since I know where it is."

Twenty minutes later, we were pulling up to this Big Ass warehouse full of all types of cars.

"Shit, I might even grab Shalil a whip."

"I knew it was a reason you wanted to come."

"If that was it I would've just said it. She been hinting that she needs a car."

"You really feeling her."

"That's my young girl, I gotta make sure she straight."

"Respect. Respect, I just don't wanna see her hurt. Shelly said that she really loves you."

"She should I've been dealing wit her for close to a year now."

"Oh, so you saying you love her too?"

"Let me say I really like her and care a great deal about her."

"But you don't love her. Naf you know a woman catches feelings faster than a man."

"How long was it before you fell in love wit Shelly?"

He did have a good point, I just recently told Shelly I love her and we been together almost two years.

"I feel you on that."

"I bet you do."

When it was all said and done I copped Shelly a 325I BMW Wagon and Trap got Lil a Buick Lucerne.

"Hey Ms. Cookie have you talk to Naf? I tried to call him, but he hasn't picked up."

"He didn't answer when I called either."

"He must be cleaning a car, he never answers when he's putting in work as he calls it."

"Is everything OK?"

"I got off early and I wanted him to come pick me up."

"I'm on my way home so I'll swing by."

"Thanks Ms. Cookie."

"Shelly you know it's no problem."

"I need to get me a car next year when I get my taxes back."

"Shit my mom and Shelly called, I knew I should of took my phone wit me." I pushed send and waited for her to answer.

"I'm glad I wasn't dying."

"My fault, I was taking care of something. What's tha matter?"

"Nothing, I was just calling to see if you had plans for tonight."

"Nope."

"Good, we're going to dinner me, you and Shelly."

"OK but I need to call her, she called me too."

"I know, she's right here wit me."

"What is she doing wit you? Is she OK?"

"Yes, she's OK, she got off early and needed a ride so I picked her up."

"Put her on the phone please."

"Hold on."

"Hello."

"Hey Sexy."

"Don't hey Sexy me."

"My bag, I didn't have my phone on me."

"Yeah I know. Meet us at ya moms house."

"I'll be there in about an hour, I need to detail this last car."

"Let one of ya workers handle it."

"Nah, this is my best customer and she wants me to do it."

"She unh unh. Do I need to come to that shop and turn it out?"

"Yeah cause you don't want that!" my mom yelled in the background.

"Yo yall trippin', I'll be there in 45 minutes."

"Nafee Symir Jackson don't make me hurt you."

"Nyshell Monai Brown you know I only have eyes for you."

"Tell me anything."

"Only tha truth Ma."

Since Shelly's birthday was in two days I decided to drop in at Dunrites to put a dub on it and then to sound of Tri-State to put a system in it. By the time, I got home it was well over 45 minutes. My mom and Shelly both had attitudes.

"Hey do yall still want to go out for dinner?"

"Where you been, it's almost 7 o'clock?"

"Last time I checked I only had one mom."

"Answer her question Nafee."

"After I finished I had something important to take care of."

"I'm sure you did," Shelly said pointing to my zipper.

"Don't turn into one of those insecure broads."

"There's nothing wrong wit being a little insecure," my mom said in her defense.

"You would know about that."

"Excuse me?"

"I said yall trippin."

"What ever, don't make me go Joey Greco on you."

"You watch too much TV."

"Who's Joey Greco?" my mom asked.

"Tha host of that show Cheaters."

(Ha! Ha! Ha!) "I've seen that show a few times."

"Look, are we still going to dinner or what?"

"We changed our mind and ordered Chinese."

"Did yall order me something?"

"No."

"I heard that," I said walking towards the door.

"Where are you going?"

"Lonestar."

"Wait for us."

"Yall ordered Chinese."

"No we didn't; we was just playing."

"Well, unless yall want to get left yall better come on."

"Who you think you talkin' to? You not too old to get ya Ass busted."

"Mom you've never beat me and I don't think you gonna start now."

"Maybe not, but I've never had a problem doing this," she said punching me in my arm.

"OOOOOW!"

"Boy that didn't not hurt." All I could do want laugh because she was right, it didn't hurt.

"Who's driving?" I asked holding my keys up.

"You are and don't turn that music up all loud either!"

"Well, I guess we'll be taking ya car then."

"If I had a car we could take mines," Shelly said being sarcastic.

"When you get ya income tax in 7 months, you can buy ya self a car."

"I sure can."

We went to the Outback instead of Lonestar and the wait was at least 45 minutes.

"Do yall wanna wait or go somewhere else?"

They both wanted to wait so I decided to sit in the truck to smoke a Dutch. As I was about to toss the Roach, Shelly came out and waved her hands letting me know our table was ready.

"You should've let ya self-air off first."

"I'm good."

"You know Ms. Cooke gonna snap."

"My mom know I smoke."

"That's not tha point, it's all about respect."

I didn't argue, I just walked back to my truck and got my Furdose that I keep in there and put some on to kill the weed smell.

"That's a lot better."

"Come on before my mom puts out an APB.

"I was just about to put an APB out on you two. *(Ha! Ha! Ha!)*

"Don't ask," we both said.

"I wasn't."

"Hello my name is Marc and I'll be your waiter for tonight. Can I get you something to drink while you look over the menu?"

"Spring water," I said.

"Sprite for me," said Shelly.

"I'll have a Long Island Ice Tea please."

"OK, I'll be right back."

"He couldn't keep his eyes off you Ms. Cookie."

"He better."

"Nafee I'm grown."

"What can he do for you working in this place?"

"I want some of these boneless wings while I wait for my food," my mom said switching the subject.

"Just like I thought."

"I know what I want."

"Me too."

"Here you go," Marc said putting our drinks in front of us, "I'll be back to take your orders."

"Nah, we ready to order now. I'll have tha Steak and Shrimp."

"What sides?"

"Mash potatoes and corn."

"Mmm that sounds good Naf, I'll have tha same thing. But instead of corn, can I have tha broccoli please?"

"Sure, and you Miss."

"I'll have tha Shimp Imperial wit extra shrimp."

"Will that be all?"

"Yeah, we straight."

"Nafee don't be rude," my mom said in a stern voice.

"How is that being rude? I just said we straight."

"He's alright, I'm like that with my Sistah's"

"Sista Wow! I'll take that as a compliment."

"You're not his Sista?"

"Try mom."

"Please accept my apology."

"For what? A compliment?"

I had to admit, dude had game like an arcade. This Nigga has my mom blushing like some young girl.

"Well, just call me if you need anything else."

"We sure will."

"Look like you got a fan Ms. Cookie."

"Yeah, me," I said with an obvious attitude.

"Naf you need to stay in ya lane. Ms. Cookie is grown she can make her own decisions."

"Thank you, Shelly."

I wasn't trying to hear that so I just kept my mouth shut, for now anyway. When we were done, my mom told Marc to bring us the check. Since I was paying mom and Shelly decided to leave a 30-dollar tip that I was sure he could use. On our way out the door, Marc stopped us.

"Here you go."

"Oh no, that's for you and tha good service we got."

"I don't need it."

"You sure? I know they don't pay a lot," I said being smart.

"I don't get paid at all; my sistah is the manager and I help her out twice a week since they are short on staff."

"You must have a Hell of a job then."

"I own my own law firm in Philly," he said handing me a card.

When I read the name I said, "Oh Shit, you Uncle Kev's lawyer."

"Kev is your uncle?"

"Yup."

"So, you're his Sista?"

"Not by blood, but yes."

"My dad was his brother."

"I've heard a lot about your dad; all good."

"Do you have a license in Delaware?"

"Yes."

"Is it cool if I give you a call tomorrow?"

"Sure, I'll actually be in Wilmington at noon. We can have lunch and talk then."

"That's what's up."

He handed my mom a card and then said, "Feel free to call me." We walked back to the truck.

"Never judge a book by its cover," Shelly said once we were in the truck.

"I normally don't, but I'm not going to let anybody hit on my mom."

"Nafee, I'm usually a good judge of character, besides he wasn't hitting on me."

"Maybe not vocally, but his eyes told a different story. Mom I don't care if you're grown or not; I'm always gonna look out for you."

"Baby you suppose to and tha same goes for me."

"Awe, a mother and son moment."

"Shelly, you always got something to say."

"That's why you love me."

I had to stop by Rash's before I went home to handle some business.

CHAPTER 17

Marc the Shark

When I walked into the restaurant I was surprised to see Uncle Kevin.

"Hey nephew, I see you met Marc tha Shark."

"Yeah, last night when he was flirting wit my moms."

"Ha! Ha! Ha! I wasn't flirting, I was being a gentleman."

"Oh, that's what you call it?"

"I call it what it was."

"I didn't come to talk about that."

"So, what did you come to talk about?"

"Putting you on retainer."

"I'm expensive."

"You say that to say?"

"Nothing, I'm just letting you know I'm expensive that's all."

"I went through tha same Shit, don't feel bad."

"I brought 30 Grand, is that enough or do you need more?"

"Nah, you good and my phone stays on 24/7."

"Imma hit my team wit ya number and they'll all hit you wit 20g's."

"Kev, you wasn't lying when you said he's all biz-ness."

"I told you I ain't got Shit on him."

"Damn and you only 17."

"I've learned from tha best."

"I do need to let you know I don't represent no Rats!"

"As far as I know I don't have no Rats on my team and if I do, you won't have to even worry about representing them."

Before we left, Marc asked me if it was alright and if he could give my mom a call.

"Marc Imma be honest wit you, I'm very protective of my mother and I don't want to see her hurt again."

"I respect that."

"I say all that to say if you hurt her you won't have to worry about representing anybody else!"

Uncle Kev said nothing just smiled and winked which let me know he'd already told Marc the same thing.

"Matter fact, let me call her and see if she wants you to have tha number." When I asked if she wanted me to give him the number, she couldn't say yes fast enough.

"Marc here's tha number, but remember what I said. Oh, if you want to make a good impression, she likes white roses. Oh, and be expecting those calls sometime today."

"Kev ya nephew is something else."

"Don't underestimate him Marc, he meant everything he said."

"I'm pretty sure he did, he's a lot like his uncle."

"On another note, I agree wit him on Cookie so if things go that far wit tha two of you and you don't think you can be that man, I would advise you to cut it off."

"Kev you've known me on a biz-ness and personal level for years' now so you should already know I don't roll like that."

"Well, now that we got that straight, what's Cleeves case looking like?"

"I don't think it'll go to trial, but if it does I'll spank it; no doubt about it."

"That's what I like to hear."

"That's why you pay me top dollar."

"Well, I'll hit you up; I need to get back up top."

"A'ight, Imma head to tha flower shop."

On my way to get the flowers I called Nafee to find out where Cookie worked so I could have them delivered to her job.

"Cookie you have a delivery up front."

"A delivery?"

"Yeah."

"I'm not expecting anything. A'ight Mrs. Margret hold me down."

"You know I Gotcha!"

"Oh, it's probably those scrubs I ordered." When I got up front I saw some beautiful roses.

"I see somebody got roses today."

"Yeah you."

"Me?"

"Yeah, they were delivered a few minutes ago."

"Are you sure they're for me?" She turned the vase around so I could see the card that was attached. I quickly opened it.

> "Hello, I was told that these were your favorite so I decided to send two dozen hope you don't mind and if you want to have dinner tonight give me a call you already know tha number."

"He must be somebody special to have you smiling like that."

"Girl, I don't even know him."

"What ever Cookie."

"Seriously, I just met him last night while I was at Outback."

"Well, at least he has good taste in food."

"He was working."

"He works there?"

"No, his Sista is a manager and he helps her out twice a week for free."

"So, what does he do?"

"He has his own firm; he's a lawyer."

"Wow, is he good looking?"

"6-1, brown skin, brown eyes and wavy hair."

"Sounds like my kind of guy; good looking and a good job."

(Ha! Ha! Ha!) "Mia, you crazy; let me get back to work."

I put my roses in the Break Room and went back to work. I couldn't stop smiling thinking about what Marc went through to send those roses. He had to get all his information from Nafee and I know that wasn't an easy task. At the end of my shift I was more than ready to leave. The first thing I did was get Marc's card out my Glove Box. After a few rings he picked up.

"Hello."

"Thank you for tha roses."

"Oh hey, I was worried you weren't going to call."

"I just got off work, besides I had to find ya card."

"Does this mean you'll be joining me for dinner tonight?"

"That all depends."

"On what?"

"If I took anything out for dinner or not."

"If you did you can cook us dinner then."

"Not on a first date sorry."

"No problem, just call me when you get home and let me know if we have a dinner date or not."

"OK." After I hung up I just smiled knowing I didn't take nothing out for dinner before I left this morning.

"I see he sent you flowers," Naf said when I walked through the door.

"Yeah, thanks to you."

"What's that suppose to mean?"

"How else would he know these are my favorite?"

"I just told him they would make a good first impression."

"What else did you tell him?"

"That I didn't want to see you hurt, Uncle Kev let him know tha same thing."

"Kev?"

"I had nothing to do wit that; Uncle Kev was there when I arrived."

"You two are something else."

"Mom, I'm gonna always make sure you straight; I put my like on that."

"Nafee, I swear you are just like ya father."

"I know, Uncle Kev tells me all tha time."

"Let me call Marc to let him know I'll go to dinner wit him tonight."

"Have a good time."

"Where you going?"

"Me and Trap gon' take Shelly and Lil to see that new movie Brooklynn's Finest wit Wesley Snipes."

"Well, have fun."

"Yeah, you too."

CHAPTER 18

Max Out

"You only got two days left now."

"I wish this Shit hurry up!"

"I got you a nice .45."

"It's on; you get something up?"

"My brother said he got a hit for us."

"That's what I'm talkin' bout."

"I told you it was on."

"Let me hit you back; I need to call Mil."

"Just hit me up tomorrow."

I had less than 48 hours before I hit the rough streets of Wilmington. I was nervous and anxious at the same time. I came to jail a young man, but now I'm leaving a grown man.

"Cam."

"Yo."

"Wilks want you at tha bubble."

"What up Wilks?"

"I know you out of here Friday and since I won't be here I wanted you to have my number in case you need me for anything." I knew he was talking about Steph my youngin who had 4 left on his nickel.

"Good looking, I'll definitely be needing you."

"I'll give you tha number when you lock in for count."

"White bag and baggage."

"Pop tha door so I can bounce." I went to Steph's door.

"Hit 8 real quick, yo I'm out," I said handing him the bag with everything I owned in it."

"Don't let nobody know you got this cell phone; Adams or Wilks will be hitting you wit tha trees. A'ight Cam be safe out there, I'm right behind you."

"Imma hold you down; I promise."

"I know you will; just make sure you keep tha flicks coming. White, do you wanna go home or not?"

"Love you Nigga," I said giving him a hug.

"You too."

"You got a visit Sunday, right?"

"Yeah, my Sista."

"Imma drop a nickel off so you can hit tha store."

"This is more than enough to hold me down."

"Fuck that, you see how I do it so now it's ya turn." I gave him dap and walked to tha out cove.

"Tha Rover waiting on you."

"Adams look out for Steph."

"You know I got him; you just stay out."

"I'll be buried by 6 than judged by 12."

"Hopefully it won't come to that."

By the time, I got to booking they already had my bag waiting. I didn't have no rap, I just put my sweat suit I brought from Commissary on and waited for them to call my name.

"White step over here." It felt good to finally get that ID bracelet off my wrist after six years.

"They finally letting you go Young Buck."

"Yeah."

"Don't come back."

"I hope I don't."

"Hey, let him out please."

It was a nice summer day out; the sun almost blinded me. My mom, Aunt Cookie, and Mil were standing out front. They all bum rushed me.

"Look at you all big," Aunt Cookie said, "you picked up some more weight since I last saw you."

My pops died when I was young so I had to man up. Nafee pulled up bump'n in this white on white Yukon Truck sitting on 28's.

"Yall gonna stand out there or get in?"

"Damn Naf, I like this Shit."

"Watch ya mouth," my mom said popping me in the back of my head.

"My bag Mom."

"You might be big, but I'll still bust that Ass." *(Ha! Ha! Ha!)*

Everybody laughed except me; I didn't find it funny.

"First thing you need to do is get outta those clothes and sneaks you can change back here," Mil said handing me a bag with a pair of True Religion Jeans, shirt and brown A.C.G. Boots.

"Cam, you hungry?"

"Yeah, let's hit Home Town."

"I need to stop by my crib to pick Shelly up."

"She so slow, she should've been ready." I pulled up in front of my crib.

"Who live here?"

"Naf and Shelly."

"Wow."

"He's done pretty well for himself over tha last few years." And just like that I was pissed off, but I tried not to show it.

"Is Shelly knocked up?"

"Yeah, she's 4½ months; I told you she was."

"You said she might be."

"Hey Cam get out and give me a hug."

"You big for 4½ months."

"Please don't remind me."

"What you having?"

"A boy!" Naf yelled.

"He don't know."

"I'm telling you, it's a boy."

"I want a granddaughter."

"So, does my mom."

"I had enough wit you two."

Once we were done eating we dropped everybody off.

"Where we headed?"

"Philly so you can get some gear unless you want to rock ya old Shit."

"You got jokes huh?"

"Nah, I'm just saying."

"Skip that Bullshit Nigga."

"Why don't you tell me I had a nephew on tha way?"

"That tells me how much you paid attention; I did tell you."

Cam was like a kid in the candy store grabbing everything in his size.

"Naf this should be enough Shit to hold me down for a while."

"You can never have too much gear."

"I know, but for right now this will hold me."

"Cam I want you to meet my man Trap."

"Where he from?"

"Originally Jersey, but he been down here so long you might as well say here."

"What part of town?"

"West side, 8th & Rodney."

"8th & Rodney?"

"That's tha same thing I said until that money started coming in."

"I want you to meet my peoples Scrap."

"Is that tha Nigga you was cell mates wit that last two years?"

"Yeah, he also Ray-Ray's brother."

"You didn't tell him nothing about me, did you?"

"Nah, just that you my brother and you got a detail shop."

"Good because Ray-Ray doesn't know who has taken all his biz-ness and I'd like to keep it that way for now."

"Scrap said Ray-Ray still got tha city in a choke hold." *(Ha! Ha! Ha!)*

"What's so funny?"

"Cam I've never lied to you about anything so I'm not going to start now."

"Listen, Ray-Ray is Damn near broke if he's not already."

"Huh?"

"Remember when I told you I had 70% of tha city?"

"Yeah."

"You probably thought I was bluffing, but I wasn't and now I got about 90%."

"Naf, why do you hate Ray-Ray so much?"

"Cam that Mafucka killed my pops."

"I couldn't believe it, but it all started making sense."

"Why is that Nigga still Fuckin' breathing?"

"I'm gonna take everything from him then Imma kill his Bitch Ass!"

"You already got tha city; what else do you want? I say let me Earth that Mafucka."

"He ain't going nowhere; I've waited 8 years' for this so Imma do this my way."

"I respect that, but no matter what I want in when you decide to send him to tha boneyard."

"You got that, but on some other Shit everything I have is half yours."

"You don't have to take anything; just be real wit me."

"I know what I did when we were kids was wrong I just wanted to do what you're doing now."

"And that is?"

"Take tha game to tha next level."

"Cam that was going to happen; you just needed to be patient."

"I was young and eager."

"All I'm saying is keep a low profile, nobody need to know what you're doing; nobody." I knew he was talking about Scrap, but I asked anyway.

"You talkin' bout Scrap ain't you?"

"Especially Scrap because one thing you need to understand, although you built a bond wit him Ray-Ray is his brother and blood is thicker than water." That was most definitely food for thought even though I knew he was right I needed to be certain.

"No problem."

"Cam, I'm serious."

"Naf, I'm on ya side; you can trust me."

By the time, we finished shopping I had dropped close to 12 Grand which was nothing. When we got in the truck a phone was ringing.

"Naf, ain't you gonna get that?"

"Shit, I almost forgot; open tha glovebox for me and grab that phone."

"Who wants to talk to me?"

"Nigga just answer tha Damn phone."

"Yo."

"What time you coming back?"

"Who dis?"

"Cam don't get hurt ya first day home."

"I know not to get no phone now," I said laughing.

"This is ya phone Naf gave me tha number." I looked over at Nafee who was sparking up a dutch.

"I'll be there in another hour or two."

"Damn Nigga, why you ain't tell me you got me a phone?"

"I forgot til it started going off."

"Naf' I need to holla at Scrap before I go to tha crib if it's cool wit you."

"I don't care, I'm not telling you not to deal wit him, just don't tell him my biz-ness; that's all."

Forty-five minutes later, we were pulling up on C.B.W.

"Aye yo, my Man, let me holla at you for a sec."

"Oh Shit."

"What up Baby?"

"Yo know…Happy to be free."

"I know that's right."

"This my brother Naf, Naf this my man Scrap."

"What up Honey?" Nafee just shook his head.

"What's up wit him?"

"He's like that, what's tha deal wit ya brother?"

"You know, trying to maintain his city."

"Is he gonna put us on?"

"He waiting on his people's."

"Take my number and hit my phone when Shit right."

"I'll do that." I hit him with my number and got in the truck.

"Cam look like ya brother doing good."

"I told you, he don't Fuck around; he got a biz-ness. Hey I'm just saying my brother got coke for days."

"Hold up," I said as I picked up my phone.

"Yo. I'm on my way."

"Make sure you hit me up; I'm bout to get me a shot."

"Imma holla at my brother and I'll hit you later."

As soon as we pulled off Nafee let me know I couldn't trust him.

"How you know that?"

"Because he lied about Ray-Ray having tha city."

"Maybe Ray-Ray didn't tell him he was Fucked up."

"I bet you won't hear from him until you call him."

"I know for a fact Ray-Ray told him Shit was Fucked up."

"How?"

"He wanted to get put on and he couldn't put him on."

"All he had to tell me was Shit Fucked up right now."

"You got a better shot at becoming President than him telling you that."

It kind of made me mad after I thought about it. Scrap supposed to be my man and he's lying to me. Already makes me wonder who can you trust? I didn't say Shit on the ride home, I just let what Nafee said sink in.

"Yo you good?"

"Yeah, I'm straight, just thinking that's all." Before I got out Nafee hit me with some real Shit.

"Cam, you my brother and that will never change. Everything I've done has been for us, not me but us. So, know that I'm wit you, not against you. If you don't believe me check ya bank account."

"My bank account?"

"Yeah," he said handing me some paperwork, "tonight we wit tha clubs up and celebrate you coming home."

"What time we leaving?"

"11 o'clock."

"A'ight and thanks Naf."

"For what?"

"All this."

"Nigga you bought that," he said winking.

As soon as I walked in the house I knew I had to get my own place.

"You finally decided to come home."

Kami had been riding it out with me for the last 18 months. Her and my mom spent so much time together you would've thought they were mother and daughter.

"Where's my mom?"

"She got called into work so it's just you and me."

"I like tha sound of that; follow me."

One hour later, I was more than satisfied with the performance Mil put on me and vice versa.

"I need to jump in tha shower; Naf will be here in a few hours to pick me up."

"Yall going clubbin'?"

"I guess, he told me to be ready by 11 o'clock."

"I can't wait til Shelly drops her load so I can go out."

CHAPTER 19

Party Time

(Beep, Beep) "That's Naf, I'll see you when I come back."

"If I'm sleep wake me up."

"Oh, I will."

(Ha! Ha! Ha!) "Boy, you funny; don't come in here all drunk thinkin' you gon' have me all sore in tha morning."

(Beep, Beep) "You better go before he be beating tha door down next."

"See you later."

"I love you Cam."

"I heard that," I responded with then walked out the door.

"Damn Naf, you ain't playing no games."

"Nah, this ya whip," he said as he was climbing in the passage side. I couldn't believe it; Nafee had gotten me a navy blue on blue Navigator on 28's.

"I don't have my L's"

"Use these til Monday. Everything is voice controlled."

I looked at him like he was crazy until he said, "Meek Mills Track 10 Volume 15."

When Meek came on to say I was impressed would be a definite understatement. How could I even think about going against Nafee after all he has done for me. I made a promise to myself that I would protect him at all cost.

"Shit look at that long ass line of people trying to get in."

"Just pull in tha parking lot."

"20 dollars."

"We want a spot up front."

"40 dollars."

"Damn Zach, it's ya people's."

He looked in the truck then said, "My bag Naf; I didn't know it was you in there. You already covered."

"You must come here a lot."

"Not really, but before we go in; put this on."

"Damn Naf."

"I had to make sure you had a little Bling."

"A little?"

"Yeah a little; hope you like it."

"I might get hypothermia from all this ICE." I had him a chain made wit his initials in ICE.

"Are you gonna look at it all day or you gonna get out."

"I was waiting on you."

"Let's go then."

"You sure you want to wait in this line?"

"Wait in line, so you became a comedian while you were locked up?"

We walked to the other side of the gate where the bouncers were standing.

"What up Baby Boy?"

"I can't call it; what's good wit yall?"

"Another day on tha J.O.B."

"Don't you mean night."

"Hold tha line up Joe. Go on in Naf."

As soon as we walked in Uncle Kev was at the counter waiting on us.

"Welcome home Nephew," he said hugging Cam.

"Now I know why we got right in."

"Of course, why should my nephews with in line at my club."

"Oh Shit! This ya place Unc?"

"One of 'em."

"You got a super long line out there."

"They all wanna see Meek and Young Chris."

"Oh, you doing it big."

"Nah, this ya welcome home party Nephew," he said handing Cam a flyer, "I don't know about yall, but I'm thirsty."

We made our way to the VIP where Uncle Kev had bottle of that Ace of Spade on ice.

"I need some Remy to go wit this."

Kev motioned for the bartender to come over. "I need you to keep tha Remy coming."

"You got it Boss."

"Make sure you have ya self a few drinks," Uncle Kev told her winking.

"You must be hitting that."

"Who ain't he hitting?"

"When you not tied down you can do that."

"Even when you tied down, you can do that," I said speaking on my behalf.

"Nigga, Shelly got you on lock."

"He don't even know huh Unc?"

"Nah, but you know he been gone for six years."

"Yeah, six long years."

"Did you get some Ass yet?"

"Come on now you disrespecting me."

"My Bag Playa Playa."

"Oh, My God there he is." We all turned to see who she was talking about.

"If it ain't my main man Kev."

"Meek what up Baby Boy?"

"In tha studio working on my CD, thanks for coming through for me."

"Kev, you looked out when nobody else did and it counted tha most we like Fam welcome home Cam."

"It's an honor to meet you I love ya music."

"We gon' turn it all tha way up tonight Philly style."

"Can ya Boy get a little shine tonight?"

"Chris, you know you can."

"Kev what tha deal Big Homey?"

"You know like Hoy said men lie, women lie numbers don't!"

"Yeah and you definitely winning."

"I appreciate you coming thru for me."

"You know it ain't bout nothing you would do tha same for me."

The barmaid brought over another 5 bottles of Spade.

"Unc can I light this up?"

"Yeah fire that Shit up."

"We drank and smoked until it was time for them to perform."

Meek started off with his classic 'In My Bag' then Chris performed some hits from his mix CD, the new print. They had the place in a frenzy; Cam was so drunk he wanted the mic. Meek gave him the mic.

"Awe Shit!" Uncle Kev and I said expecting the worse.

"When it's all said and done Cam be tha last man standing, blunt in my mouth, arm fully extended, hand still clutching tha Cannon Rapid Fire Gunz spittin' so fast you thought they was speakin' Spanish caught a six year did for hittin' a Nigga in his leg came out a grown man, but went in as a kid."

I looked at Uncle Kev while he just tore the stage up. When he was done, they went crazy.

"Yo Cam you nice. How long you been writing?"

"A few months."

"Damn, you sound like you been doing it all ya life."

"Kev, you need to get him in tha studio."

"Nah rappin' ain't for me."

"If you ever change ya mind tell Kev to get at me."

I took a mental note to talk to Cam that was another way to clean up this money. For the rest of the night we hung out with Meek and Chris in VIP getting smashed. By the time, it was time to leave Cam was pissy drunk.

"Yall a'ight to drive or yall want to stay up here?"

"Noooo I need to go home or Mil gonna pitch a Bitch," Cam said with slurred speech.

"Imma call Shelly and have her call Mil."

For it to be two in the morning it was humid outside.

"Hello."

"Hey Babe, sorry to wake you."

"Naf are you drunk?"

"A little bit."

"Unh, unh your drunk; you know you not a drinker."

"I know but Cam's home."

"Oh My God, if you're like this I know he's drunk."

"Yup."

"Where is he?"

"Uncle Kev got him."

"I hope yall not driving home tonight?"

"Yeah."

"No tha Fuck you not Nafee!"

"Hey, hey chill out Baby."

"Chill out my Ass, I'm not having my son grow up wit out his father because you decided to drink and drive."

"I don't want Cam to get in trouble."

"Don't worry about Mil, I'll call her. You just make sure yall don't drive."

"Shelly."

"Yes."

"You said son."

"That's because you say it so much it rubbed off."

"Shelly."

"What Boy?"

"I love you Boop-Boop."

"I love you too; now bye so I can call Mil."

"It's still early let's hit another spot."

"What Shell say?"

"She's gonna call Mil so we good."

"Well, in that case let's party til ha sun come up."

"Imma have my Young Boy drive."

"Nah Unc I'm good to drive you know I know my limit."

"A'ight then follow me, we gon' go to this spot that stay open til 6."

We got in the truck I hit the stash box pulled out the bag of sour diesel that was inside.

"Damn you on some James Bond 007 Shit."

"Just being safe. And strapped," he added pulling out the .40 Cal that was in there.

"We ain't gon' need that, not tonight anyway."

Long story short, we partied until 5 in the morning and then we went to Uncle Kev's house and crashed.

CHAPTER 20

Untrustworthy

It had been two months since I have been home and Shit has been lovely.

"Aye Naf, you was right."

"About?"

"I ain't heard from Scrap since that day we seen him over eastside."

"I told you that."

"I know but that was my Man 50 Grand in tha bing."

"That's how it always goes; let me ask you something."

"I'm listening."

"How long was he home before you got out?"

"2 months."

"How many times did he get at you?"

When I didn't say Shit Naf said, "That's what I thought."

"Cam that right there should've let you know what type dude he was cause I know if I'm in tha cell wit a Nigga for 2 years' I don't care if I got out 2 weeks before him Imma get at him."

"Let me ride through east and see if he's out there."

"Waste of time, but go head."

"Damn Homey what's really good?"

"Cam what's up?"

"I ain't heard from you."

"I just got back in town last night, my brother had me down VA running one of his spots."

"Why you ain't hit me? I would have went down wit you."

I hope Cam know this Nigga lying like a Mafucka.

"I see ya Peeps got a new truck."

"Nah, this my Shit. My moms bought it as a coming home gift."

"Daaaamn must be nice."

"Nigga stop frontin' I know Ray-Ray hooked you up."

"Scrap why you didn't hit my phone?"

"You know I was outta town."

"When you leave cause you been over my house all week."

"You need to leave them dippers alone."

"What Mafucka? Don't try to play me in front of ya friends," she said walking away with attitude.

"She be high off them dippers trippin."

"So, what's tha deal wit you? Is it on yet?"

"I'm waiting now, I'll hit ya phone in a few." I knew he was lying because I had changed numbers and he didn't know it.

"A'ight I'll hit you."

"Now do you believe me?"

"All he had to do was keep it real. If his brother Fucked up, he Fucked up."

"Naf I would hope if you was fucked up you would tell me."

"Yeah, I would, but you ain't never got to worry about that, trust me."

"I always do."

"Did Aunt Cookie tell you about tha surprise party for my mom?"

"I was going to ask you about that."

"I overheard her tell Aunt Cookie about these earrings and diamond bracelet she wanted."

"I was going to get her this Gucci handbag I know she likes."

"Tha one like Shelly's"

"Yup."

"Why don't you get her one of those Sharpay Dogs?"

"Naf she don't have time to take care of no dog."

"I don't know it's up to you."

"Cam I know you upset about ya boy but understand and know this, as long as you got me you don't need nobody else."

"I know I just can't believe I let this Nigga play me."

"It happens."

"Not to me Naf not to me."

I knew what that meant so I defused the situation and I said, "Maybe I'm wrong; maybe you can trust him."

"Only one way to find out."

"I'm listening."

"Imma tell him I got a job and where tha spot is. Imma even put 5 stacks and 4½ in there but Imma tell him we gon hit in 2 weeks." I sat there and smiled because that's something I would do.

"Cam, drop me at tha crib; I gotta go wit Shelly to tha doctor's office."

"A'ight, I gotta take care of something anyway."

As soon as I dropped Naf off I hit Scrap.

"Yo who this?"

"It's me Nigga."

"Damn you changed ya number."

"Yeah, I had to; anyway, where you at?"

"On tha 9."

"Stay there I'm on my way I need to holla at you."

Fifteen minutes later, I was pulling up on C.B.W.

"Cam what's good?"

"I can't call it Doc; what's good wit you?"

"You know me, trying to get some of this twenty money."

"I heard that."

"You look like you eating crazy."

"Nah, me and my brother got a detail shop out Newport."

"Oh Shit! Sparklin' is yall Shit?"

"Yup." Scrap jumped in.

"Imma holla at you Doc."

"No doubt, be easy."

"I don't like that Nigga."

"Doc good peeps."

"Fuck that Nigga."

"Damn, yall from tha same block."

"Just cause we from tha same block don't mean I gotta Fuck wit him."

"You right."

"So, what you need to holla at me about?"

"I put him down wit my bogus heist, but told him we had to Nah 2 weeks before we hit."

"Where is tha crib at?" I told him where the spot was at and he smiled.

"I'll hit you next week so we can go over it again."

"A'ight just hit me I'm around," he said getting out my truck. Now all I had to do was wait.

"Hey Ray-Ray."

"What up Scrap."

"My man just put me on this caper that's pose to be worth some change."

"You mess wit him like that?"

"We was locked up together, but Fuck 'em."

"I know where tha spot is so we can hit it tonight."

"What about ya man?"

"What about 'em?"

"That's all it is then."

"Be ready by 10 o'clock."

"I'll meet you at Dads."

"Don't bring Jimmy, this between us."

"This might be tha hit I need to get back in position again."

"You never found out who was in control of all this product that has tha city in an uproar?"

"I know tha product is coming from my uncle, I just don't know who's moving it."

"Maybe we need to corner a different market after this hit."

"What are you suggesting?"

"I think we need to mess wit heroin."

"Nah, that Shit makes you hot fast."

"Yeah, but tha turnover is crazy; besides all we need is six months, no more."

"I don't know."

"Just think about it."

Later that night, I met up with Ray-Ray.

"You ready?"

"Let's do it."

We rode to the house listening to Pac's 'Hail Mary' for some reason whenever I was about to do something I always listened to that.

"Park around tha corner so nobody will see us."

"Don't look like nobody's home."

"Good let's get in and get out so I won't have to body nobody."

Damn I should've known, Naf was right. This Mafucka is a Snake and I need to cut the grass. I stayed there until they came out; got what I needed and then pulled off. I stopped at Aunt Cookie's to holler at Naf.

"How you know we was here?"

"I talked to Naf and he said yall would be wit ya big stomach."

"Shut up Boy."

"Now is that any way to talk to ya son's uncle?" I asked rubbing her stomach.

"Naf, Cam is here."

"Hey Cam."

"Hello Aunt Cookie."

"I just got off tha phone wit ya mom, she thinks we're going to a play next weekend for her birthday."

"Good she doesn't suspect anything."

"Cam, I'm in tha basement; come on down and get that head cracked."

When I got down there he was playing that Wii boxing game.

"Grab the control."

"Nah, I don't feel like doin' no sweating. Look at this," I said passing him my digital camera.

"Wow! I told you."

"Damn, didn't you just put him on today?"

"Yup."

"He ain't waste no time and look at Ray-Ray. Did you put that fake coke and money in there like I told you?"

"Yeah, a booked-up Brick and 50 Grand of Funny Money."

"Now that you got proof he can't be trusted you still want to Fuck wit 'em?"

"Don't disrespect me, I got another plan."

"Cam I know we ain't always seen eye to eye, but I would never steer you in tha wrong direction."

"I know and Naf I gotta be honest; at one point I wanted to take everything from you."

"Why? I held you down."

"I know; I just felt like I should've been me on top."

"You were."

"Nah, I wasn't you were; you did what I couldn't. Take tha game to tha next level."

"As long as I was on top you was too."

"I know you more than proved that."

"Well, that's tha past; no need to dwell on that."

"You're right and I'll holla at you tomorrow. I'm pose to be taking Mil to tha movie."

"Movies?"

"Yeah, she wants to see Why Did I Get Married Too."

"I got that on bootleg and it's clear as Shit."

"Word. Let me get it for tha night."

"On ya way out ask my mom if she's done wit it."

"A'ight."

On my way upstairs I stopped in the middle of the stairs.

"Aye Naf."

"Yo."

"I love you Bro."

"I love you too and don't be getting all mushy on me."

"Fuck you!" I yelled back walking out the basement.

"Oww Aunt Cookie"

"Well, don't be cursing around me."

"I didn't know you were standing there."

"Well, now you do."

"Ahh ha," Shelly said smiling.

"Aunt Cookie are you done wit that movie Naf left."

"Why Did I Get Married Too?"

"Yes."

"Yeah, let me go get it for you. Who you watching that wit, Mil?"

"Nah, my young jawn."

"Yeah, what ever."

"Then why you ask a dumb question you knew tha answer to?"

"Because I can, that's why."

"I see you still go that Smart-Ass mouth."

"Sure do."

"I hope you don't pass that along to my nephew."

"If he does, he better know how to fight."

"Come on Mom you know Imma teach him how to box just like dad taught me. I knew it, I Fuckin' knew it." Aunt Cookie smacked me upside my head again.

"Next time it's going to be my fist in ya mouth."

"I'm sorry, but I knew Naf knew how to box that day you beat Titus up. Why you ain't tell me?"

"Because I knew you would want me to teach you and you don't have no patience."

"You right, but I would've had some for that."

"You say that now, but trust me; it was days I didn't want to train but I had to."

"He still trains," said Shelly.

"I've been doing it for eleven almost 12 years' so it's like part of my everyday routine."

"Well, I wanna be included. You know for tha past 6 years' I've been doing a little boxing myself."

"I'm in tha gym by 8 o'clock every morning."

"I'm up at 7 working out anyway."

"See I've done it all and frankly Girl I'm tired of this emptiness. I wanna belong to you and only you."

Phone Rings…

"Hello."

"I'm leaving my Aunt Cookie's now."

"Damn Girl he's coming!" Shelly yelled.

"On my way…Bye."

"You gotta nerve tha way you blow my phone up."

"Sooooo Whhaat! But you love it."

"Hit me in tha AM Naf."

"I Gotcha Baby Boy!"

"Oh, I almost forgot; Shelly can you go wit Mil tomorrow and find a nice crib?"

"About time, I thought you would never leave tha nest."

"I almost said something to you Naf."

"I wish you would've," Aunt Cookie said with her fist balled up.

"That's my cue to go…Love yall."

"And we love you back," Aunt Cookie said.

That night after we watched the movie, I thought long and hard about what I was going to do about Scrap.

"Baby, Baby."

"Huh?"

"You OK? You was in another world just now."

"I was just thinking about some things Naf said to me earlier."

"You wanna talk about it?"

"Nah, but I did ask Shelly to accompany you tomorrow wit finding a house."

"I was calling her and Lil anyway."

"Lil went outta town wit Trap."

"No she didn't, I just talked to her. They'll not leaving til next week."

"You sure?"

"Yeah, she has to take this exam in school in 2 days."

"Have you decided what you're getting ya mom for her birthday yet?"

"Nah, I'm still debating if I should get her that dog or not."

"Get it."

"Huh?"

"Get it, she was just saying that once you move out she was gonna buy herself a dog. So get her tha dog."

CHAPTER 21

The Set Up

"First we gonna work out for an hour, then we'll box."

"No problem."

First, we hit the bench and I was shocked when Naf threw up that 325. I didn't want to show off so I left the 325's on there and did 10 reps. Once we were done he showed me a few combinations and some footwork.

"No, No like this. Keep ya shoulders leveled." *(Jab, Jab, Jab, Combo, Jab, Combo, Jab.)* I couldn't front, Naf definitely knew his Shit.

"That's enough for today. Now let's get on tha treadmill and run for 45 minutes."

"You do this every day?"

"Yeah, except Sundays."

"And you been doin' this for 11 years?"

"11 years' faithfully."

"I definitely have a new-found respect for you; my workouts ain't Shit compared to this."

"Come on, let's get outta here."

"Ray-Ray just hit me wit 20 Grand, you keep everything else."

"Do you think ya man will know you hit it wit out him?"

"Nah, and if he do Fuck 'em. I'll send his Ass to tha boneyard wit out thinking twice."

"Hold up, this him now."

"Hello."

"Yo what's up?"

"I can't call it; waiting on you so we can do this hit."

"Somebody beat us to it."

"Are you serious?"

"Yeah, but I got something better for us anyway."

"How soon can we do it? My brothers out of town and a Nigga hurting."

"I'll be thru later wit all tha details."

"Cool."

"He said he got another hit for us since somebody beat us to tha other one."

"Dumb Ass Nigga."

"I told you I knew he would be useful; now I just gotta wait for him to come thru."

"This Nigga must really think I'm dumb."

"Yeah, I bet him and Ray-Ray getting a laugh outta that."

"Imma have tha last laugh."

I filled Naf in on what I planned on doing and he wanted in. Later that night, I went by to scoop Scrap up.

"So what's tha plan?"

"We gonna hit tha crib now."

"Now!"

"Yeah, unless you got something else to do then I'll do it solo."

"Nah, I'm wit you, I just need to get my heat."

"I got you covered, only thing we gotta put these on," I said handing him a mask.

"Why we need these?"

"I found out who been running ya brother outta biz-ness." He looked at me like how did you know.

"Come to find out it's my brother."

"Oh Shit!"

"That's tha same thing I said when he told me. Then tha Nigga has tha nerve to tell me about this spot that he keeps no less than a hundred grand."

"Is anybody there?"

"Nah, probably just him."

"Sweet."

"I don't wanna hurt him, but if Shit gets hectic I'll hit him in tha leg or arm." We pulled up down the street from the house.

"Come on…don't put ya mask on til we get on tha porch." Once we hit the porch I knocked on the door.

"Who it?"

"Pizza delivery."

"Why yall always knocking on my door? Down tha street," he said snatching the door open.

"Oh Shit!" he said trying to snatch the door shut.

"Listen don't make this no harder than it has to be."

"Yeah Nigga, just tell us where everything at so we can route."

"Ain't nothing here."

"Well where is it?" I asked knowing what he was gonna say.

"It's all over my man Ray-Ray crib."

(SMACK) "You lying Mafucka!"

"Yo Nigga what tha Fuck you doing?"

"This Mafucka is lying through his teeth."

"My Man just tell us where it is." He gave us the address to the spot that they just hit.

"Stop trying to play us."

"I'm not."

"Yes, you are; now either start talking or die," Scrap said putting the gun to Naf's head.

"You know what, let's cut tha Bullshit," I said snatching my mask off.

"Cam what tha Fuck are you doing?"

"Take ya mask off Scrap."

"Well, Well, if it isn't tha Thief himself."

"What you talking about Naf?" He passed me my digital camera. I looked as if it were my first time seeing it.

I turned my gun on Scrap, "Nigga you tha one who hit that spot."

"What spot?"

"Nigga don't play dumb," I said showing him the pictures of him and Ray-Ray.

When he didn't say Shit, I said, "Damn, I thought I could trust you. Nigga we shared tha same room, sink and toilet for 2 years. Nigga I even fed you."

"Naf, you was right." Scrap had his gun pointed at me as well.

"One of us is gonna die and it's not gonna be me," Scrap said pulling the trigger. *(Click, Click, Click)*

"Did you actually think I was gonna give you a loaded gun?" He lunged forward and I caught him with a straight jab putting him on his pamper. I saw Naf screwing the silencer on his gun.

"My brother said you couldn't be trusted that's why I set you up wit tha dummy hit." The look on his face said it all.

"Yeah that Brick was booked up and tha 50 Grand was Funny Money. If you would've kept it real you could've been on top, but since you didn't you gon' die."

"My brother isn't gonna let you get away wit this."

"Don't worry about ya brother, he'll be joining you soon enough."

"Do you know who my brother is and tha power he has in this town."

"Let's be real, ya brother is broke and has no power. That ended when I got into tha game 6 years' ago. I took all of his biz-ness next Imma take his life."

"He never did Shit to you."

"He made an enemy outta me when he killed my pops."

"If yall gonna kill me then kill me."

"Ya wish is my command," Cam said taking the gun and pulling the trigger until the clip was empty.

"What are we gonna do wit his body?"

"Leave it, wipe down anything you touched." Naf was starting to pour gasoline all over the house.

"You gonna burn down ya house?"

"This Ray-Ray's house so Fuck 'em." He lit a match and threw it on Scrap's body which instantly flamed up. We walked out without being noticed.

Nafee just looked at me and then said, "At all cost."

I understood exactly what he meant so I responded with, "And Vice Versa."

CHAPTER 22

One Down

"Thanks for inviting me; this is a nice party."

"Marc you don't have to thank me, I wanted you to come; I enjoy your company."

"I enjoy yours too."

"I would hope so; we been dating for a while now."

"Hey Mom Marc."

"What up Naf?"

"Did you get that new Jaheem CD yet?"

"Yeah, I copped it yesterday; it's definitely gonna go platinum."

All that was code for did you get that money from Trap and the rest of the team. At first I didn't want my mom seeing him or any other man for that matter, but I couldn't let my selfishness get in the way or ruin my moms happiness.

"I'll let you two talk, I need to find Jonda."

"I know that's ya Aston Martin outside."

"Yeah, I already thanked Kev so thank you too."

"For What?"

"Yall paid for it." *(Ha! Ha! Ha!)*

"You funny, but you're right so you're welcome."

"Marc tha Shark, what up Baby Boy?"

"What up Cam?"

"I can't call it."

"This a nice party you threw for ya mom."

"You of all people should know how we do Shit."

The DJ put on this old cut by Whodini called Friends. My mom, and everybody else went crazy.

"Come on Marc lets dance."

"I would love to keep chatting, but I gotta go."

"Naf this must have been tha Shit back in tha day; look at 'em."

"I know, but look at those two," he said referring to Mil and Shelly.

"Come on, let's show them how to party."

By the end of the night everybody was partied out; especially my mom, Aunt Jonda, and Ms. Porsha. Before we left my mom opened her gifts; she had gotten everything from clothes to diamonds.

"Baby thank you for tha necklace and earrings! How did you know?"

"I have my ways."

"Mom I got one last gift for you," I said walking to get it.

When my mom saw the big box she said, "Baby what is in that big box?"

"Open it and see." As soon as she opened it she screamed.

"Oh My God! How did you know I wanted a Sharpay? Come give ya mom a kiss."

"I love you Mom Happy Birthday."

"This has been tha best birthday ever; yall out did ya selves."

"Is it a boy or girl?"

"Boy."

"Then I'll call him Capone."

"How old is he Cam?"

"3 months."

"Un oh Ms. Jonda, you gonna be shampooing ya carpet a lot until you potty train him."

"Was it hard to potty train Sash?"

"Not really, he'll get tired of pissin' and having his nose put in it."

"Aye Naf it's still early, let's hit tha highway."

"Cam I was hoping we could spend some time together tonight."

"You're welcome to come wit us if you want."

"Why don't you come over my house, we can watch some movies and talk."

"OK cause I'm partied out for one night."

"You driving, or am I?"

"You are, I always drive."

"Well, give me ya keys Naf so we can leave."

"Don't be getting drunk to tha point where yall can't drive."

"I ain't doing too much drinking tonight so I'll be cool."

"Naf you ain't no drinker anyway." We said our goodbyes and then hit I95.

"Who tha Fuck would do some Shit like this?" He was beefing with them Cats from the hill.

"He did tell me one of them said he would burn together wit you in Hell."

"Who tha Fuck said that?"

"He didn't say."

"Come on let's pay them Niggaz a visit."

"Jimmy I swear somebody gonna die behind this."

When we pulled up on 3rd & Clayton it was packed. I could remember at one point we would pull up and Mafucka's would flock like birds to us. And now they act like we don't even exist.

"Yo there go that chick that won me that 10 Grand."

"Zina, Fuck her."

"After winning me that money she's a'ight wit me."

"I bet she is."

"Ain't that Corey over there?"

"Yeah."

"Aye yo Corey, let me holla at you for a sec."

"Hold up."

"Who tha Fuck do he think he is?"

"Corey come here Nigga!"

"Nigga I said hold tha Fuck up!" By now everybody was looking on.

"This Nigga got me Fucked up," Ray-Ray said pulling his .45 out.

"Ray-Ray chill one time, just went across Rodney."

"Yo what's up? I was handling important biz-ness."

"Don't get too big for your britches."

"What's that suppose to mean?"

"Just what I said!"

"Ray-Ray I don't owe you."

"Nigga you forgot who put you on?"

"How could I forget about tha way you was charging too much for that Bullshit Yola."

"All Bullshit aside, sorry about what happened to ya brother."

"That's what I came up here for."

"I don't know why? We ain't have nothing to do wit that."

"But you know who did."

"Nah, can't say I do."

"Well, pass tha message, when I find out who did it; they're dead."

"Yeah, a'ight."

"Jimmy, did you see how everybody was watching us or was it just me?"

"Nah, it wasn't just you, I peeped it too."

"I know that Nigga know something; he just not talking."

"He'll talk don't worry."

Ray-Ray just leaned on the truck not saying a word. *(Pop, Pop, Pop, Pop)* Shots rang out and everybody scrambled in every direction. We jumped in the truck and pulled off slowly not to cause any unwanted attention to ourselves.

"Did you see who was shooting?" My phone rang with an unfamiliar number on the caller ID.

"Hello."

"I'm on fire! She's burning up. If I hit her with a Cardier it'll cool her down. I'm on fire! She's burning up. " The line went dead.

"Oh, these Mafucka'a think this Shit is a game."

"Who was that?"

"I don't know; they just let that Faith & Freeway track play."

"What track?"

"Burning up. Hold up…Hello."

"Next time it won't be shots in tha air." *(Click)*

"These Mafuckas Fuckin wit tha right one."

"What they say this time?"

"Next time shots won't be fired in tha air."

"We'll go back thru when tha sun sets."

"Yo you know ya boy came through here a little while ago."

"Who my Boy?"

"Ray-Ray."

"Fuck that Nigga."

"Was he trying to off that Bullshit Yola?"

"Nah, he was asking Corey about his brother."

"What's up wit his brother?"

"You know he got set on fire in one of Ray-Ray's houses."

"Nah, I didn't."

"Yeah, he was burnt so bad that they didn't know it was a body. If you ask me I think Ray-Ray set tha house on fire to collect tha insurance but didn't know his brother was in there."

"I wouldn't put it past him."

"Be on point because he'll probably be back thru when tha sun goes down."

"We'll be waiting on him too."

"He don't understand his time is over and nobody's scared of him."

"Well, if he come back wit that dumb shit, he won't be leaving alive."

"Cooter do me a favor."

"What's that?"

"Don't kill him."

"Why not Naf?"

"Imma be tha one tha sends him to tha boneyard."

"How bout' if I just hit him up a little?"

"As long as you don't kill him."

"Gotcha!"

"Trap ya young boy Cooter is a wild cannon."

"Since he been getting at a dollar he calmed down a lot."

"He's a loyal little Nigga if he Fucks wit you, but if he doesn't then that's another story."

"I gotta swing by Lil's to drop this money so she can get something to wear for that party down tha River Front."

"I forgot all about tha bosses wear suits, diva's wear dresses party."

"So, that means you ain't cop nothing yet?"

"Nah."

"Me Either."

"Let me call Cam, if he ain't grab nothing we can shoot up New York tomorrow to tha Gucci store."

"All you wanna wear is Gucci."

"Hey if you got it why not wear it."

"I heard that."

I called Cam but he was already in Phil with Mil getting something to wear. When we got to Lil's Shelly was there.

"Damn. Look at you."

"How many months are you now?"

"7½"

"Hey Baby."

"Hey."

"How much do you need?" Trap asked pulling out a wad of money.

"I don't know? It depends how good you want me to look." All I could do was laugh.

"Naf, can Shelly go wit me and Mil?" I looked at Shelly who just smiled and hit me with that look that she knows I can't resist.

"Let her go Naf she ain't been out since you found out she was pregnant."

"I know but you know how Niggaz get at a party sometimes."

"Lil, I told you he wasn't going to let me go."

"Since you don't have nothing to wear you might as well go to New York wit me and Trap tomorrow."

"New York?"

"Yeah Lil, New York."

"Well, count me in cause I know Imma find some hot Shit."

"We leaving at 8 o'clock."

"I hope they got something to fit me," Shelly said rubbing her belly.

"I'm sure they will."

"I'll see you later at home."

"OK, don't forget to get Sash's food."

"I'm bout to do that right now."

"Yo man Shelly look like she bout to drop any day."

"I know."

"You didn't really want to let her go did you?"

"Not Really, but I'll just be on her hip to make sure her and my son straight."

That night Cooter said Ray-Ray never came back thru. I still told him to be on point. The next morning I was up at 7 o'clock.

"Shelly if you plan on going you better get up and get ya self together."

"I'm up."

"Un oh."

"What?"

"You got that look in ya eyes."

"What look?" she asked knowing exactly what I was talking about but I told her anyway.

"That I want sex look."

"Because I do."

"I told you I don't wanna hurt tha baby."

"And I told you my doctor said you won't."

Since I was backed up I ended up giving in. Shelly was just as backed up as I was; she had multiple orgasms in less than 15 minutes.

"Wheeeew, thank you Baby I needed that badly."

"Happy to oblige; now let's get cleaned up."

Thirty minutes later, we were waiting for Trap and Lil to pick us up.

(Beep, Beep)

"Baby go head, let me use tha bathroom before we leave."

"Trap, Lil."

"What up Naf, hey Naf."

"Where my girl, I know you didn't change ya mind about her going?"

"No, he ain't change his mind, I had to pee."

"Naf she got her piss jar cause we not stopping!"

"Yeah right, if I gotta go we stopping!"

"I know that's right," Lil added. Me and Trap started begging up.

"I don't know what's so funny."

"Trap give me a light."

"You not smoking that around Shelly." I started laughing again.

"He do it all tha time, it don't bother me."

"My nephew don't need to be getting high though."

"Ya mom smoked wit yall and yall came out half Ass a'ight."

"OOOWW!"

"Lil don't be punching my baby."

"I know you ain't say that when I'm taking up for you. Naf pass tha weed."

"I know you ain't gonna smoke around Shelly," Trap said mimicking Lil.

Shelly fell asleep half way there. When we finally got to New York we were all starving so we stopped at Kentucky Fried Chicken.

"Ya son was really hungry tha way he was kicking me."

"He like his dad, he like to eat."

"Naf, where tha Gucci store at?" I hit him with the directions and within 20 minutes we were there.

"This is a big store."

"Girl who you telling Damn."

"Excuse me Miss do you have anything that will fit me?"

"Yes, over there in our Maternity section."

"Damn, Gucci has a Maternity section? Talk about being lucky."

"Come on Naf, help me pick something out."

They had a lot of stuff that I knew would look good on Shelly. I always tell her she looks even sexier pregnant. She was self-conscience because she gained 15 pounds, but if you ask me, she gained it in all the right places. Shelly tried on this red Gucci dress and I was in awe at the way she looked in it.

"Damn Baby, I don't know if I want you to go now."

"Now you got me blushing."

"It's tha truth."

"Baby Imma get a few things."

"Do you."

When it was all said and done, I ended up spending a nice piece of change.

"Trap we better get outta here before Naf ends up trying to buy tha store."

"I think you're right Shelly."

"Hey Naf, you ready?"

"Hold up, she went to see if she had these in my size."

"I'm feeling those Baby."

"Me too, that's why I'm getting them."

"You so Damn Smart."

"Maybe just maybe that's why I graduated top of my class."

"Go head rub it in."

"Awe, I'm sorry Boop-Boop."

"Will yall two cut it out and come on." We hit a few more stores.

"So, this is where they get those fake Air Ones from?"

"Yup and everything else that's bootleg."

"I know, I'm bout to buy a box of White T's so I won't need none for a minute."

"Before we leave I wanna holla at my cousin about some sour diesel."

"Nigga I'm all for that, let's roll."

"Unh, uhn, unh, that's a Damn shame."

"I know yall don't make no since."

Trap's cousin had pounds of sour diesel for the low so I copped two and told him I would be in touch. We didn't say it in front of the girls, but we were both thinking the same thing; start selling weed.

"WE ALL WE GOT BROTHERS FOR LIFE, WE ALL WE GOT, WE ALWAYS DO WHAT'S RIGHT BROTHERS FOR LIFE."

"Yo what up Cam?"

"Yo yall still in tha Big Apple?"

"We on our way back now."

"Good cause ya boy Ray-Ray on some Wild Wild West Shit."

"Did anybody get hurt?"

"Two people got hit, nothing life threating."

"A'ight, Imma hit ya phone as soon as I get in town."

I had about enough of Ray-Ray it was time to show him who was in control. Trap knew something was up without me saying anything. He just gave me that look through the rearview. I called Cam as soon as we hit the city.

"Yo meet me at tha Greenville spot in 25 minutes."

Trap dropped us at the crib and then let me know he would be there as soon as he dropped Lil off.

"Naf is everything a'ight? You been mad since you talked to Cam."

"One of tha employee's at tha shop Fucked somebody's car up."

"I'm sure it will be a'ight."

"You probably right, but you know how I am when it comes to my shop."

"I hope ya son don't inherit ya attitude."

"I don't have an attitude, I'm just not going for tha Dumb Shit!"

"You gonna be OK, I need to get to tha shop."

"Yeah, I'm about to go to my mom's for a little while."

"You want me to drop you off?"

"No cause when I'm ready to go I don't wanna have to wait."

"Ya mom will bring you home Naf, I can drive I'm only 7½ months; it's not like imam go in labor."

"If you say so."

"Boy I'm glad we having a boy and not a girl."

"Why is that?"

"You would be to over protective, that's why."

"I might have to agree wit you on that."

"Might."

"OK I'll agree."

(Ha! Ha! Ha!) "You funny, but I love you."

"I love you more."

"I seriously doubt that."

Before I left out I put my weed up, but not without taking me an ounce to smoke.

"Naf, I remember a time when you didn't even like to smoke, now that's all you do."

"I pay for it and no I'm not being smart."

"What took you so long?"

"You know how Shelly is."

"So, what's up wit this nigga, why is he still alive?"

"Look, this is what we gonna do."

I devised the plan and everybody was more than happy to carry it out. We all went to the Gold Club since we knew on Friday's it would be the spot to catch him.

"Yo, I never understood why somebody would waste their hard-earned money on these broads. Don't get me wrong, I've tricked a little bit of doe at one of these places a few times, but believe me it was well worth it."

"You must have been at a night on Broad or tha Bath House?"

"Cam, you must of been there yourself."

"I Plead tha 5th."

"Look who just walked in tha room."

"This is going to be easy, he's by himself."

"Hey Sady, keep 'em coming."

"Rough day Sweetie?"

"Rough ain't tha word."

"Where's ya friend tonight?"

"He had a date so it's just me."

"OK, I'll be right back."

"COMING TO THE STAGE IS LOLA!"

"I'm in love wit a stripper. Damn Shawty must be new I ain't never seen her before, wow she definitely knows what she's doing that for sure," he thought to himself.

"Here you go Sweetie." I was so turned on by Lola I didn't hear Roxy.

"That's tha new girl; she just started tonight."

"She may be new in here, but she's not to this stripper game." I was amazed how she had her ass cheeks dancing to the music as if it was natural.

"Look at that Nigga, he bout to cum all over himself. I told you my cousin wasn't not joke."

"Is that tha one from Atlanta?"

"And you know it."

"If she wasn't ya folk I might've had to try her out."

"Nigga she grown; she calls her own shots."

I watched as she walked over to him, did a split, and made her Ass bounce like a nigga was dribbling a ball. Once she was done, she went to the back to change into something else.

"Damn, I gotta have her tonight. Ms. Sady tell her to come holla at me when she's done."

"Sure thing, Sweetie."

Then minutes later, Lola come from the back with a pair of Short Boy shorts, a half shirt that read "TASTY".

"I know you are."

"Excuse me?"

"Ya shirt."

"Oh?"

"What a nigga got to do to get a taste of you?"

"Pay like ya weight."

"That ain't bout nothing," I said pulling out my knot.

"A'ight Playa; let me finish my shift then we can hang out."

He thought to himself, "Just thinking about what I was gonna do to her had me hard as a brick."

"Hey Cuz, he's all for it."

"OK, here's tha room key. We'll already be waiting, just call when you're on ya way."

"Gotcha Cuz!"

I smacked her Ass and winked at her to let her know I was definitely feeling her. Feeling her especially after that performance she just put on.

"You can get me free of charge," she whispered in my ear. I tapped her on the Ass when she walked away.

"Sorry Trap, but Imma definitely get a piece of that before she goes back to tha A."

"Do you...just don't fall in love and then be calling Shelly talkin' bout you ain't coming home on some Harlem Night Shit."

(Ha! Ha! Ha!) "Yo, you funny Dude." After a few more shots we got outta there.

It was the end of my shift and I was tired as Hell, but I wasn't going to let a free 10 Grand go by. When I walked outside dude was standing by this black truck.

"You driving?"

"Yes, so follow me. I already got a room." She must of knew she was getting into something tonight.

I followed her to the Marriott by the airport in Philly. We went to the elevator, took it to the 4th Floor and then went to Room 409.

"Did you bring some smoke?"

"Never leave home wit out it."

"Smells like you already got some good green."

"That's sour diesel you smell, I smoked that before I went to work. So, if you don't mind me asking, how long you been dancing?"

"Too long. Look let's cut all tha small talk; I want 1500."

"You must be top notch."

"I'm willing to bet tha whole 1500 that I'm tha best you're ever and will ever have hands down."

"I'll take you up on that bet."

"Take all your clothes off while I slip into something more comfortable."

"Why don't you just get naked, they coming off anyway."

"You right. I hope you don't mind being tied up."

"Not at all."

We watched as she took out two pair of handcuffs.

"Damn, you a real Freaky Bitch."

"Ms. Bitch to you!"

Once she had him cuffed and gagged it was our turn.

"Well, Well, Well, if it isn't my man Pots in Pan." He was talking, but wit those thongs in his mouth it was muffled.

"Take those thongs out his mouth."

"Trap what tha Fuck you think you're doing?"

"I knew I shouldn't have trust this Bitch!

"You were thinking wit tha wrong head."

"What do you want wit me?"

"We want you to deliver a message to Ray-Ray."

"Who's we?"

"Us," I said coming out the bedroom with Cam behind me."

"Hold up, ain't you Scraps boy?"

"I was until he tried to play me so I dealt wit him accordingly."

"That was you?"

"Nah, that would be me."

"You look like this guy I use to know."

"Samad?"

"Yeah."

"Everybody says that and I should, that was my dad until Ray-Ray Bitch Ass killed him."

"That was…" *(He cut him off)*

"I know 8 years' ago. That's why I've been working so hard to take everything from him."

"So, you're tha one who's been…" *(He cut him off again)*

"Yup. That's been me taking over tha city."

"You'll never get away wit this."

(Ha! Ha! Ha!) "I already have. First, I'll take all his money and then I'll take tha things he loves."

"Do you know what's gonna happen once I tell him it's been you all this time?"

"Nigga, unless a dead man can talk you won't be telling Shit!"

"Help Somebody! Help Me! Toya slit him from ear to ear.

"Bitch Ass Nigga doing all that yelling like some broad. Take those cuffs off, wipe this whole room down, and let's get tha Fuck outta here."

Before we left I put 3 shots in his head just as a statement.

"What time you gotta be home?"

"I'm grown, I go home when I get ready."

"Or until tha wife call ya phone."

"If you say so."

"Well, let's get a room."

"We don't need no room, I got a couple of spots."

"So what we still standing here for?"

"Yall go head, I'm riding wit Toya."

"Remember what I said Naf," him and Cam both laughed.

"Did I miss something? Let me in on tha joke."

"Naf will tell you."

"Ya cousin crazy."

"You just now figuring that out?"

"Yeah."

"So, what was tha joke?"

"You not going to let it go are you?"

"Nope."

"He told me not to get all Harlem Night."

"I heard that."

Shelly hit my phone as soon as I got to the crib to tell me she was staying at her moms. That couldn't have worked out better.

"Gotta go home huh?"

"You must didn't hear me tha first time, I'm grown." Toya did Shit to me that I've never had done, I had to put work in so I could hit it the next time she came to town or I was in the A.

"Damn Boy, I thought you was going to be a minute man, boy was I wrong."

"They say never judge a book by its cover." I pulled out my phone.

"Who you calling?"

"Baby I love you, but I ain't never coming home."

"Boy you stupid."

"I know you got them Niggaz in tha A going crazy."

"Believe it or not, I had a 8-year relationship that ended 11 months ago and this is my first encounter since."

"After 8 years, what went wrong if you don't mind me asking?"

"He moved to California and tha long distance thing wasn't working plus I think he was doing him anyway. Now don't get me wrong, I had friends, but nothing sexual. How long you been wit ya Girl?"

"3½ years."

"Do you love her?"

"Yeah."

"Then what do you call this?"

"I dibble once in a while."

"And I was hoping to do this again."

"Oh, don't worry about that, when are you going back home?"

"Sunday."

"Did Trap already pay you ya money?"

"Half of it."

"You didn't have to kill him I was going to do it."

"I know but I couldn't stand to hear him yelling like some broad being robbed.

"Ya dude was a fool to let you go."

"I know, wasn't he?"

We got into it until the sun came up then we showered.

"You wanna grab some breakfast?"

"Sure. Why not?"

"I know this spot we can go to."

"I don't wanna get you in no trouble."

"For having breakfast wit my cousin?"

"I heard that Cousin."

After breakfast Toya drove me back to my car.

"Maybe I can see you later, if you not too busy."

"Sure, that'll work."

"Where you staying?"

"At my aunt's house, why?"

"I thought you were staying at tha motel, I was going to let you stay here til you leave."

"I might take you up on that."

"Here's tha keys if you decided to and this is my number, call me when you get time."

"Imma spend time wit my aunt then I'll call you."

"Shelly, Shelly…*(No answer)* she must still be over her mom's house."

I took another shower, got dressed, left her a sweet note, and then went to the shop.

"I didn't think you was coming in today."

"I'm not tha average nigga, give me some credit."

"Naf I gotta kept it 100 wit you, my Cuz hit me and said she thinks she's in love."

"Yeah, what ever."

"Real rap. I told her that you already got a wifey so fall back."

"She can be my mistress."

"Naf don't get caught up, I've been in this situation before so believe me when I say it never ends good."

"Trap Toya lives all tha way in Atlanta."

"I know, but I'm telling you trust me Naf."

"How long you think it'll take before they find Jimmy," I said switching the subject.

Trap looked at his watch and then said, "They already have."

"I think we need to hire more workers, biz-ness is booming."

"Put a 'HELP WANTED' sign in tha window."

"Nah, I know a few young boys who could do tha job well."

"Call 'em up, tell them to be here in tha next hour."

"No problem."

"I'll be in my office, I have a little paperwork to catch up on."

I couldn't get Toya off my mind no matter how hard I tried or what I did.

"Naf."

"What up Cam?"

"How was she last night?"

"Let's just say any nigga would be a fool not to wife her."

"That good?"

"You couldn't imagine."

"I need a shot of that then."

"She's not going to give you a shot."

"How you know?"

"She don't get down like that, but you can try."

"Damn Tender Dick Ass Nigga, you Fucked up already?"

"Nigga I ain't Fucked up," I said, "try."

My phone started to ring, but I didn't recognize the number so I started not to answer. However, when I remembered I gave Toya my number.

"Yo! Who this?"

"Is that how you answer tha phone?

"It is when I don't know who's calling."

"Stop giving ya number out so much then."

"I don't."

"Mmm Hmm tell me anything."

"Is that why you called to get smart wit me?"

"No, I called to see if you were busy."

"Something like that, tha shop is packed right now."

"Do you work in a barber shop?"

"No, I own a detail shop."

"Where at? Cause my car needs to be fully detailed."

"Do you know how to get to Newport?"

"I was born in Wilmington; I moved to Atlanta."

"So, I'll take that as a yes." I gave her the location and then hung up.

I don't know what it is about him, but I'm feeling him something terrible. I already was going to have my car cleaned so why not go to his shop. He wasn't lying, when I pulled up it was cars everywhere. I felt all the eyes burning a hole right through me and why not, I'm drop dead beautiful. Toya was 5' 6", with a caramel complexion, hazel eyes, shoulder length curly hair, and an ass that would make Beyoncé' jealous. Not to mention, she was rocking a peach Christian Dior sundress with matching sandles and well manicured toes.

"Hey Cuz."

"Hey Toya."

"Is Naf still here?"

"Yeah, he's in tha back, I'll get him."

"No need, I'm right here. No wonder all these niggaz are drooling at tha mouth, you look amazing."

"Thank you. You not looking too bad ya self." To me I was basic; in pink Gucci Khakis rolled up, a white Gucci V-neck, white Gucci sneaks with no socks.

"We bout to change his name to Gucci."

"Gucci?"

"Cuz that's all he wears."

"Cut it out. I wear other stuff too."

"Yeah, but most of tha time its Gucci," Cam added.

"Well, I want tha full detail from top to bottom."

"I'll put Skip right on it. Which car is yours?"

"Tha cream 645."

I had to go look, I thought the Honda she was driving was hers.

"Nice car, I see you got taste."

"I like to think so. Can you wax and shine my rims for me?"

"That's how we do it anyway."

"Excuse me."

"Matter fact, I'll do ya car myself, just to make sure it's spotless."

"You don't have to do that."

"I know I don't, but I am. Let me change."

I looked at Trap, "You offended him when you said to wax tha rims."

Naf came back out in a pair of Jordan shorts, Wife Beater and

Jordan on his feet.

"Let me get the keys please."

"I thought I was going to talk to you while I got my car cleaned."

"You can still do that. I know how to multi task." We talked while I hooked her car up.

"All done. Would you like a little fragrance inside?"

"Sure, why not." I hit her with a little Black Love.

"Wow! Them niggaz in tha A ain't got Shit on you Naf. How much do I owe you?"

"A night of club'n and call it even."

"That's no good, I was gonna ask you if you wanted to hit Philly tonight anyway."

"Well in that case, just a kiss on tha cheek."

"You are too sweet, too bad you are taken or I would take you back wit me tomorrow."

CHAPTER 23

Down Ass Chick

My whole world was crashing down around me. First, my brother now Jimmy.

"What tha hell was Jimmy doing at a hotel in Philly?"

"I told him tricking would be tha death of him one day, I just didn't know it would be this soon."

"Jimmy tricked so much it's hard to pin point who could have set him up." My phone went off, but since I didn't know tha number I didn't answer. Whoever it was they were persistent.

"Hello."

"You're next Nigga!"

The phone went dead. I tried calling the number back, but the number wasn't in service. How could that be when they just called from that number? I needed to lay low so I decided to stay at my house out in Hockessin for a little while or at least until I figure out who's behind all of this. When I got to my car, there was a note on my windshield.

"YOU CAN BE TOUCHED AT ANY TIME BITCH NIGGA!"

I quickly looked around, but didn't see anyone or thing out of place. I was skeptical about starting my car so I checked for any bombs or anything that might be out of place. Once I was certain it was cool. I started my car halfway expecting it to blow up. When it didn't, I pulled off, checking my mirrors every few minutes to make sure nobody was following me.

"Yo, let Naf know that's been handled."

"Call his phone."

"I did, he ain't answering."

"A'ight, I'll let him know."

"Aye Trap, what did Naf have Spank doing?"

"You got me, but I think it had something to do wit Ray-Ray."

"I wish he just kill that Nigga and be done wit it."

"I told him tha same thing."

"You trying to hit Samba tonight or you chilling wit Lil?"

"Nah, we can hit tha club if you want to, I just gotta change clothes."

"Me too."

"I'll pick you up in about an hour."

"Cool."

"Toya, you ready?"

"Just about. Give me 5 more minutes." Toya came down looking like a breath of fresh air.

"So, that's how they do it in tha A?"

"No, this is how I do it where ever I go."

"I heard that," I said staring at her in this sky blue Badgley Mischka dress that left nothing for the imagination and a pair of sky blue Christen Louboutin open toe shoes. And if that wasn't enough, then her diamond necklace, bracelet and earrings definitely sealed the deal.

"Stop staring at me like that."

"I think I need to change."

"Boy, you know you look good." She was right. I did know I looked good with cream linen pants, a linen sky blue Button up and cream & sky blue slip ons, all Gucci of course.

"I like those glasses."

"Thank you.

"So, you ready?"

"Hold on, I need to run upstairs real quick to grab something." Naf came back down with this diamond necklace on that he could light up a dark room with.

"Now you showing off."

"Nah, this how I do it."

"Where we going?"

"Tha Convention Center; they having their Summer Jam/Players Night Out."

"We might be under dressed for something like that."

"We cool. Too bad you leaving tomorrow because next Saturday Doc B. is having a Bosses Wear Suits, Diva's Wear Dresses party. Now that they coming wit that Shit on."

"Trap was telling me about that, I might come back up for that wit a few of my girlfriends." We smoked a few dutches on the ride up.

"Have you ever taken an e-pill?"

"Nah, I heard about them through Cam and Trap."

"Want one?" she asked pulling out a sandwich bag with some in it, "it won't hurt you, I promise you'll like it. I use to be tha same way til I tried one."

"Give me one."

"Take this blue Dolphin." Fifteen minutes later, I was parking the car in Pennicie's Lot.

"I'm taking my weed wit me this time."

"You can smoke in there?"

"On tha roof top."

"See we not under dressed."

"Yeah, I see. We blend right in. I need a drink."

"First round on me."

"Nah, you good, I got us tonight."

"Let me find out you one of those niggaz that don't want a female to pay for Shit."

"Since I invited you it's only right." We hit the bar and then took a couple of pictures.

"This place is big." Toya had a lot of admirers checking her out which only made me smile.

"Why you smiling?"

"All these niggaz sweating you."

"Like you need to talk," she said pointing to a group of females that were staring me down.

"That Shit don't mean nothing to me, I'm here wit you."

"Well, at least for tonight you belong to me," she said leading me to the dance floor.

WE UP IN THE CLUB. I SEE HER DO HER THING. YOU MIGHT WANNA RAP. BUT SHELL MAKE YA SING. SEE I WAS ON HER. BUT SHE WAS ON HIM. SHE ALL UP ON MY THING. I GOT

MY THING ON HER HIP.

"This my Shit right here!" *HEY! LIL MOMMA SO HOOD. I LOVE YA GIRL. LIL MOMMA STAY FLY. I LOVE YA GIRL.*

Toya was doing her thing with heels on. Not to be showed up, I was with her step for step.

"Wheeew, I need a drink now."

"Me too, that e-pill must of kicked in cause I was feeling like I was tha Shit and nobody could tell me otherwise."

"Two double shots of Remy straight."

"Make one on tha rocks please."

"Somebody can't hand I see."

"No somebody's gon' have to drive home."

I don't know if it was the e-pill or liquor, but I was horny as a Mafucka and Toya wasn't helping by grinding all over me.

"I see somebody is excited."

"Yeah, so don't move til he calms down." *(Ha! Ha! Ha!)* We both had to laugh at that.

"Let's hit tha roof top so we can blow some of this good green."

"Come on," she said grabbing my hand leading me toward the roof top.

"Damn Shawty Fat to death."

"Excuse me," I said stopping to see who was going to man up.

"Nigga you heard me," I said, "she Fat!" Before I could respond Toya was pulling me toward the roof top.

"I don't give a Fuck if you My Girl or not a Mafucka ain't gonna disrespect me or you."

"Naf, that Shit ain't bout nothing."

"It's one thing to stare, but to say that Shit when we walking by especially when he been eyeing you all night."

"Don't let it bother you."

"For me not to say Shit, would be saying it's OK to disrespect me and that's not OK."

"Light tha Dutch up; Fuck 'em."

No soon as I lit the weed, him and his boys came out and stood behind us. Toya stepped in front of me and then turned me around so they wouldn't try nothing.

"Wanna go to another club?"

I looked at my watch it was only 10 o'clock, "We can, it's up to you."

"Come on then, let's go," she said mean mugging dude.

He looked at his two boys and then said, "We out too."

I knew it was going to be some Shit, I just had to make it back to the car. I heard him tell his boy they were parked by us so when we got to the car it was on.

"Naf, did you hear them?"

"Yeah, but don't worry; I got a surprise for all three of 'em."

About half a block behind us I knew I had time to get to my pistol. When we reached the car, I told Toya to get in while I talked to them.

"Unh, Unh, I'm not leaving you out here by yourself."

"Toya trust me please."

"Aye Shawty you look to good to be wit this lame Ass Nigga."

"Only a lame nigga would stalk a broad who was wit another nigga all night."

"Now who really tha lame nigga?"

He acted like he wanted to throw a punch so I pulled out on him. *(PIT, PIT, PIT, PIT, PIT, PIT)* Before he could say anything else I hit all three of them two times in the chest and then calmly go in my car and pulled off.

"Silencer?"

"Yup. Whenever I go out I always bring it that way if something like that goes down it won't be heard."

That whole scene made me respect Naf even more and from that moment I knew I wanted to be in his life at all cost.

"You know I was gonna bust a cap in they Ass," she said pulling out a 25.

"No, but I did know you would have my back if need be."

"Naf, I know we just met yesterday, but it seems like I've known you forever."

"That's crazy cause I feel tha same way."

"One thing about me, I keep it real Naf."

"And so, do I."

"I'm not trying to break up no happy homes, but I am feeling you."

"Imma be honest because that's all I know how to do. I love my girl and I would never want to hurt her but I'm also feeling you as well."

"So now what? We just let it play out; I mean you live in Atlanta and me here so it's not like we'll be seeing each other often."

"Yeah, you're right," I said out my mouth, but my brain was clearly thinking I'll be visiting a little more now that I have a reason to.

"Why don't we skip tha club and head back home."

"They say great minds think alike."

"Fuck we can't even get to our car, they got tha parking lot taped off. I knew we should've went to Samba or Palmers instead of coming here to Pennicle."

"Cam, you wasn't saying that when you was inside partying ya Ass off."

"You right about that," I said dapping him.

A police officer was asking everybody if they saw or heard anything.

"How about you two, did you see or hear anything?"

"We just came out and I need to get to my car so I can go home."

"I'm afraid that won't be…"

"Officer Sams."

"Yes LT."

"You can let everyone get to their car." Neither of us said anything, we just walked to our car.

"Samba don't shut down til 4 and it's only 2:15. What you want to do?"

"Nigga why ask a question you already know tha answer to, you know tha way."

"OOOOOOH NAF YEEEEES, YEEEEES, AHHHH OH MY GOD I'M CUMMING! Damn Boy you trying to really put it down. OOOOOH I'M CUMMING AGAIN, YEEEEES! That's my spot right there."

He was definitely handling his business; he had me nutting back to back to back, nonstop. I normally in control, but not this time; he wouldn't let me get it together. I muscled everything up in me, turned him over and rode him like the true CHAMP I am.

"Damn Toya, it feels good."

"Cum for me then Daddy." With that he starting trembling.

"Oh Baby, I'm Nutting." I jumped off him just in time to catch the whole load in my mouth without missing none.

"I don't know what you trying to do to me but Damn." We fell asleep, woke up, went at it again and then fell back asleep.

The next time we woke up it was 8 o'clock.

"What time you leaving?"

"10, 10:30 at tha latest." She read my mind, rolled over and it was on for another hour. After she showered, we kissed and then said goodbye.

When I turned my phone on I had all kinds of messages. After checking them I started with the most important ones.

"Hey Baby, I was worried about you, I haven't talk to you in 2 days."

"Didn't you get my letter off tha fridge?"

"I haven't been home, but I got ya message you left on my answering machine." Hearing Shelly's voice kind of made me feel guilty about the last two nights I spent with Toya.

"You still at ya moms?"

"No, me, Lil and Mil are on our way to Hometown to get a bit to eat."

"Call me when you're done, I thought maybe we could spend some time together. A'ight I love you Nafee."

"I love you too."

I decided to head home for a shower and change my clothes. No soon as I got out the shower my phone started to ring. Without looking I picked it up.

"Hello."

"Hey you," All I could do was smile.

"Nice to know I can put a smile on ya face."

"And vice versa."

"You almost home?"

"About 6 hours away."

"Maybe next time you should just fly."

"I rather drive, that way I won't have to get no rental."

"You could always drive Traps truck."

"Neggy Boop-Boop? I'd rather drive one of my own.'

"So you got a few whips huh?"

"Just this one and another one."

"I didn't want nothing, just called to check up on you."

"I'll hit you when I hit tha A."

"A'ight drive safe."

Damn hot line. "Hello."

"Bout time, I been trying to reach you since yesterday."

"I was tied up."

"We got ya boy under surveillance, he's been hiding out in this house in Hockessin that he thinks nobody knows about."

"Just keep laying on him."

"Naf just let me earth this nigga so I can get back to getting my money."

"NO!"

"Say no more."

"Imma pay you for ya time trust me." I hung up and thought about how I was going to put that dog out of his misery.

Over the next few days I couldn't get Toya off my mind. I didn't call because I didn't want to seem like a stalker. My thoughts were interrupted by the sound of my phone...

"Yo."

"Hey stranger."

"Hey, I was just thinking about you."

"I can't tell, you ain't been calling me."

"I didn't want to seem like a stalker."

"Oh, I see, let me be tha stalker."

"It's not like that."

"Then how is it? Tell me cause I'm surely listening? Hello, hello."

"I'm here."

"Well, please tell me how it is."

"Toya, like I told you, I'm really feeling you but I don't think it's fair that I have a girl. You deserve more than that."

"Naf, I appreciate tha concern, I really do. But let's be honest, I knew what it was from the door so if I don't have a problem wit it, neither should you!"

"You didn't even let me finish what I was saying."

"Well finish then."

"I'm just going to let it play out."

"I thought we had already established that before I left.

"What's ya...Oh never mind, I'll get it from Trap."

"Get what from Trap?"

"Don't worry about it." We talked for another 45 minutes and then said our goodbyes with the promise to call one another later.

"Damn Nigga...What you smiling so hard for?"

"Ya Cuz is crazy as Hell."

"Naf, I see where this is headed so just be careful."

"I am Trap. Why couldn't I have met Toya 3 ½ years' ago? She's every niggaz dream wifey."

"Toya has been more like a Sista than a cousin to me; we been through a lot of Shit together."

"She's definitely a ride or die mommy."

"I know...I wasn't surprised when she slit Jimmy's throat."

"Yeah and when we went out I had to body these three niggaz in Pennicie's Parking Lot and she was ready to ride out wit a nigga."

"Holy Shit!"

"What?"

"That was you who killed them niggaz that night."

"Yeah, they disrespected me and Toya."

"Nah cause we was in Pennicie's and when we came out they had Shit taped off."

"What's Toya's address?"

"Why you ain't ask her?"

"Cause I didn't want her to know I was sending her flowers."

"She's got you open too."

"What do you mean me too?"

"She said you got her all Fucked up and she can't explain it." All I could do was smile knowing we were both Fucked up. As soon as I got her address I called and had 3 dozen white roses sent to her.

"Girl, whoever he is, he got you all Fucked up. I know I've never seen you like this, not even wit Evan."

"Did I show yall tha picture of him?"

"No Bitch, let us see!" I ran upstairs to get the picture I had blown up of us at the Convention Center.

"Damn, is he mixed wit something?"

"No, he's all Black."

"Bitch, he is sexy; he could be a model. Does he have any friends is all I need to know?"

"He only Fuck wit Cam, his brother and Trap."

"Oooh ya Sexy Ass cousin?"

"Yup."

"Next time you go back up there I'm going."

"Me too."

"Well they got this big party going on next weekend."

"Bitch say no more we there."

(Ding-Dong)

"Shonie get that please."

"Hello I have a delivery for a Latoya Cray."

"Toya." When I got to the door and saw all those roses I couldn't believe it."

"Sign here please."

"Evan is really trying to get back."

"He can forget it, we're over."

"You don't want them?"

"Hell No!"

"I'll take "em," Shonie said opening the card, "uh I think you want these."

"No I don't want 'em."

"Let me read this then you can tell me if you still don't want 'em."

"I don't want to hear what he has to say."

"Trust me, you do."

"Shonie just read it," Angel said getting frustrated.

```
    Hey there Beautiful,
    I couldn't get you off my mind so I decided
to send you some flowers. Hope I didn't overdo
it, but I wanted to put a smile on your face
like you do mines whenever I think about you.
    Love, Nafee
```

As soon as I heard Naf's name I jumped up and started screaming, "Bitch you must of put it down for him to send you all these flowers!"

"Didn't you say he was from Delaware?"

"Yeah."

"Are you sure he has a girlfriend?"

"Yeah."

"Well, I would be trying to get her out of the picture."

"Angel you know you can't do it like that."

"You gotta play tha mistress and eventually he'll choose you over her."

"Tell her again Shonie."

"She already knows how it goes."

We need to hit the mall so we can show these Delaware broads how us Bitches from the A do it.

CHAPTER 24

Back from the A

"I gotta get outta this house, I've been cooped up for 3 weeks now. If a nigga want me, then he can come get me." I went upstairs put it on my bullet proof vest and then rolled out.

"Yo tha Rabbit is finally coming out of tha hole."

"Should we call Naf?"

"Nah, let's just following him first."

The first stop he made was on the hill to cop some dippers and then he went to his baby mom's house over eastside.

"I don't know why Naf don't just put him next to his brother and be done wit it."

"Put this on his windshield and pull down tha block."

I watched in the rearview as he came out read the note and then looked around all nervous.

I grabbed the paper off my windshield. And just when you thought it was safe to surface!

"Damn! They must of been waiting on me to come over here." I got in my car and made sure both my guns were off safety.

"Come try that Shit if you want, I promise somebody is coming wit me." A tap on my window cause me to jump.

"What you jumping for Nigga?"

"That Shit will get ya wig pushed back," I said exposing my two .45's.

"Fuck you so jumpy for Nigga?"

"It's a lot of Bullshit going on."

"Yeah, I heard about Jimmy. You a'ight?"

"I'm good."

"Well, be easy, I gotta bust this Trap." I looked around before pulling off.

"Hey Girl what's up?"

"Doesn't look like I'll be going to tha big party this weekend."

"Why not?"

"My doctor put me on bed rest."

"Are you serious. Why?"

"Yes, because my blood pressure was kinda high."

"Well, I guess I won't be going either."

"I can't not let you go because of me."

"You don't have no say-so in the matter." *(Ding-Dong)*

"Get that, it's probably Mil."

"What yall talking bout?"

"We're not going to tha party Saturday."

"What? Why not?"

"My doctor put me on bed rest because of my blood pressure."

"We going to watch some movies."

"Well, I'm not going if yall not going."

"I know Naf going to be mad; all he's been talking about is how good I'm going to look."

"Cam too."

"Don't get me started on Trap."

"They gon' have to be okay wit some stuff."

"Let's all call them now." We all picked up our phones and called. All our phones went off at the same time.

"Hello," we all said in unison.

After five minutes, we were all off the phone.

"That couldn't have worked out better," Cam said with a smile.

"Mil said she wasn't going to the party because Shelly's doctor put on bed rest."

"Lil said the same thing."

"You Niggaz look like yall mad."

"Nigga only reason you ain't mad is cause Toya gonna be there."

"Yeah and two of her girls."

"She didn't tell me she was bringing friends."

"I know she's bringing Shonie wit her."

"She said, her girls Shonie and Angel."

"I don't know about yall two niggaz, but I'm cool wit Shelly being on bed rest; I didn't want her to go anyway."

"That's crazy."

"Only reason I didn't want her to go is because she's pregnant, no other reason."

"That's what ya mouth say."

"Hey man, I don't gotta prove nothing to you."

"Did you collect that money from them niggaz on tha ave?"

"Not yet?"

"Well, you need to handle that; Kev will be down in a few hours."

"Don't worry, I Gotcha!"

"Trap, you get at them young boys on 5th?"

"Yeah, but I gotta holla at Wap and his Boys."

"You think you can holla at ya cousin about that sour diesel?"

"Imma call but he gonna have to find a way to get it to us."

"Especially tha money we gonna spend wit him."

"Shit, he might come down on tha number depending on how much we spend. Matter of fact, let me call him now..."

"What tha deal Cuzzo?"

"Same Shit, trying to get this paper."

"How much you want for 10 pounds of that sour diesel?"

"$25,000, but if you grab 20 or better, I'll let them go for 2 stacks a piece."

Naf gave me the thumbs-up and then made a 5 with one hand and 0 with the other, "That's cool, I need 50. How soon can you get 'em to me?"

"If you want me to bring it all tha way to you it's gonna cost an extra 2 stacks."

"Like I said, how soon can you get it to me?"

"First thing in tha morning; just give me tha address where you want it." Once he had the info he said be expecting it between 6 and 7 tomorrow morning.

"Let everybody know on ya end you got 'em for 5 stacks a pound since they want 6,500."

"Imma holla at my young boy on 7th & Washington so he can flood up there."

"Aye we can also flood 24th; get that block back jumping again."

The next morning Trap was waiting on the package which arrived at 6:30. We spent the morning busting down the work.

"I don't know about you but I'm starving."

"Let's go to J Farmers on tha mall." My phone went off causing me to smile.

"Hey you."

"Hey you ya self."

"I'm looking forward to seeing you and two days."

"I wish you were coming up today."

"Be careful what you wish for."

"What's that suppose to mean?"

"I'll be there in tha next hour, I'm coming thru Baltimore now."

"Yeah," I said not believing her.

"Yeah, me, Shonie and Angel."

"Hey Nafee!" I heard them yell in the background.

"Tell 'em hi."

"He says hi yall."

"You miss me?"

'Toya stop asking a question you already know the answer to."

"If I knew tha answer I wouldn't ask." Park right here Trap."

"Where yall at?

"Uptown at J Farmers bout to bust a grub."

"Is Cam wit yall?"

"No, he's at tha shop."

"Angel can't wait to meet him. Where you gonna be in 45 minutes?"

"Probably at tha shop."

"Okay, I'll call you in 45 minutes."

"I'll be waiting."

"Naf I can't wait to have you inside of me."

"That's makes two of us."

"Well, I'll call you in a little bit.

"Yo is you gon' talk on tha phone or come in and get some grub?"

"You sound like a broad."

"What ever, lunch is on you Honey," he said putting his hands on his hips.

"Yo you stupid."

We walked in to find Ray-Ray standing in line.

"If it ain't tha coolest nigga in Nebraska."

"What up Trap? I heard bout' Jimmy; how you holding up?"

"Hey man, I'm a soldier."

"I see you got a little Samad wit you. What tha deal Youngin?" I didn't say Shit, just stared at him.

"Shit Youngin, I know you ain't still holding on about ya pops." I wanted to shoot him right there.

"You look like you want to try me; better come correct," he said showing his two .45's.

"I'm tha least of your worries."

"What's that suppose to mean?" he asked walking towards me.

"Aye Ray-Ray you might wanna fall back."

"Oh, I see, you got tha young buck under ya wing hustling for you."

"Nah, this my peeps."

"Well in that case, why don't you come work for me." Ha! Ha! Ha!

"What's so funny?"

"Why would I want to hustle for you? You're broke with a capital B."

"If you believe everything you hear, you're just as dumb as ya dad."

He grabbed his food then walked towards the door; before he walked out he turned and said, "If you ever disrespect me again, I'll make sure you lay next to your pop!" That was it; I walked outside to put some hot Shit in his Ass but the police were standing out there.

"Ray-Ray make sure you kiss ya mom and tell her you love her tonight." I got in the car wit out sayin' another word.

"You forgot ya food."

"I lost my appetite, take me to the shop." I went straight to my office and slammed the door.

"You two Niggaz arguing again?"

"Nah, him and Ray-Ray got into it."

"What?" After Trap told me what happened I made my mind up; Ray-Ray was history.

"Hey Cuz."

"Toya, I thought you wasn't coming up til Friday?"

"Changed my mind."

"Hey Trap."

"What's up Shonie?"

"Is that all you see?"

"Hey Angel."

"Oh."

"Shonie, Angel this is Cam."

"You wasn't lying when you said he was sharp."

"Where Naf at?"

"He in his office, he's pissed."

"He didn't sound mad when I talked to him earlier."

"A little incident happened right after yall hung up."

"Let me go put a smile on his face." **(Knock, Knock, Knock)**

"Come in."

"Hey Daddy."

"Oh Shit. What you doing up here?"

"I told you I was an hour away."

"I thought you was playing."

"Hell Nah, I couldn't wait to see you."

"Shonie and Angel wit you?"

"Yup, they out there flirting."

"Wit Cam and Trap I hope."

"Of course."

"Trap said you was pissed about something."

"I was until you came in."

"I was hoping to put a smile on ya face."

"You always do."

"Do I?" she said standing up and locking the door.

"You so nasty."

"I been waiting to do this for tha past two weeks."

"Is that right?"

"Sure is," she said lifting her dress exposing that she had no panties on.

"You're crazy."

"I just need 10 minutes." She wasn't lying, 10 minutes later we were both Cumming and we made our way to the bathroom.

"Ain't nothing like a quickie." *(Ha! Ha! Ha!)*

"You sound like a nigga saying some Shit like that."

"Come on before they come in here."

"So what happen that had you so pissed off?"

"That, cocksucker Ray-Ray."

"Is it something you can't handle?"

"Nah, his days are numbered and he don't even know it."

"So this is Mister Nafee that has my girl all Fucked up?"

"Shonie shut up!"

"Hey I call a spade a spade."

"And so do I; that's why I told my Cuz what you said."

"Bitch stop lying."

"Ya picture don't do you justice."

"I hope that's a good thing."

"Sure is."

"Trap did you get somebody to wash my baby?"

"Yeah, you good except that dent on tha side."

"What Fuckin dent?"

"Calm down, I'm joking."

"I was gonna snap."

"Ain't nobody doing nothing to ya 645."

"That ain't no 645; it's tha new S600 on deuces."

I had to look out the window, "Excuse me."

"You're excused."

"Let me find out you down Atlanta hustling."

"Yall already got something to wear for tha party Saturday?"

"And do."

"You know you gotta come wit that Shit on."

"Trap don't disrespect us; if nobody else, you should know how we do it."

"Stop taking everything to heart, you sound like somebody else I know."

"Fuck you Nigga."

"Guilty conscience?"

"Not at all."

"So, Fellas what's on tha agenda for the night?"

"2 dollar Tuesday."

"Count us in."

"Cuz yall staying at mom's?"

"Nah, we gonna stay at the Hotel DuPont."

"I see you got money to blow"

"Oh, so you don't wanna stay at my spot?"

"I didn't wanna just invite my friend's without you saying it was cool."

"Whenever you come in town you and whoever you wit are more than welcome to stay there; unless you got a nigga wit you."

"Don't disrespect me, I don't get down like that."

"Don't take it tha wrong way but I'm not ya man so you can do what you want." I could tell she caught an attitude cause all she said was come on yall, Cuz I'll hit you up later; rolled her eyes at me and then left.

"You pissed her off Naf."

"By telling tha truth? I don't want her to think that she can't do her."

"Evidently she doesn't wanna do her."

"All I know is you better not have Fucked it up wit Angel for me."

"Cam, what I eat don't make you Shit; you should know that by now."

"Girl, did you hear him talkin' bout I'm not ya man you can do what you want?" Angel and Shonie didn't say anything, they just looked at each other and smiled.

"Looks like somebody is falling in love."

"Bitch ain't nobody falling in love; watch ya mouth."

"Such hostility."

"Toya you can be mad, but I respect him for that."

"She's right; how many niggaz wit a girl would say something like that? Most niggaz want they cake and eat it too. Wifey at home under control and then they want to control tha side piece also."

"Toya let me ask you a serious question."

"What?"

"We all like Sistahs, so keep it real; why are you really mad?"

"Shonie I honestly don't know."

"Well, I do so, Imma tell you," Angel said with a big smile.

"True you only known him for a few weeks, but you have fallen for him to tha point you don't want to mess wit no other nigga. Maybe you should just tell him how you really feel so yall can be on tha same page."

"Hold that thought," I said answering my phone.

"What up cuz?"

"This ain't Trap."

"Why you call from his phone?"

"I didn't think you would answer mines since you left wit an attitude."

"No I didn't."

"Yes you did."

"OK, maybe a little one."

"Look, I wasn't trying to be smart; only honest."

"I know and I probably just took it tha wrong way."

"Toya all I was saying was that since I have a girl it wouldn't be fair to say you can't have friends or see who you wanna to see."

"Have you took tha time out to think that maybe I don't want any friends?

"Let me hit you from my phone Trap needs his phone." He hung up and called me right back.

"Naf I can't explain it but I'm really feeling you."

"That goes both ways; I just don't want you to get hurt."

"I'm not coming into this wit blinders on. Not to mention, I'm a big girl I can handle myself."

"So does this mean we can still stay at ya house?"

"I never said you couldn't."

"That's what I'm talkin' bout."

"What?"

"You got a smile back on that pretty face."

"Boy you a mess."

"Yall get settled in and I'll hit you later."

"A'ight."

"You back smiling, he must have said what you wanted to hear."

"He just put everything in perspective for me and I have to admit he ain't like no other dude I've ever met."

"How old is he?"

"He'll be 19 next month."

"He is very mature to be 18."

"You gon' to jail."

"Angel shut up, he's legal."

"Toya's a cougar." *(Ha! Ha!)*

"I'm only 24; you act like I'm 35 or something."

"How old is Cam?"

"19."

"Oh My God, I'm a cougar too." We all laughed hard.

"At least we can save some money staying at his house."

"Turn that up, that's my Shit!" ***TAKE THIS PILLOW RIGHT HERE I KNOW YOU EXCITED IF YOU BITE IT THEY WON'T HEAR.***

"That Trey Song is something else talkin' bout tha neighbors know his name." We pulled up to the house took our bags in to get settled in.

CHAPTER 25

Finished

"Where yall at now?"

"Just pulled up to his spot in Hockessin."

"What's tha address? I'm on my way."

"I hope tonight is tha night we off this Faggot."

"Me too, I'm tired of babysitting this Nigga."

Thirty minutes later Cam was pulling up.

"Yo what's tha deal, is he still in there?"

"Yeah, probably high on them dippers."

"I'm bout' to end this little charade, it's gone on long enough."

"I've been trying to tell Naf that for a while."

"Is that tha pizza man going to his house?"

"Yeah."

Cam jumped out, "Excuse me excuse me."

"Yeah?"

"How much do I owe you for my pizza? I was about to run to tha store when I saw you pull up."

"14.95."

"Keep tha change."

Thanks." Once the pizza man pulled off Cam knocked on the door.

(Knock, Knock)

"Who is it?"

"Pizza delivery." I could hear the chains coming off.

"How much do I owe you Youngin?"

"$20." I could tell he was high from the way he was sweating.

"Do you have change for a 50?"

"Yes," I said reaching into my pocket and coming out with my 9 with the silencer.

"Hold up Youngin."

"Nah, you hold up and back up."

He tried to turn and run. *(Pit! Pit!)* Two shots ripped through the back of his legs.

"AAAAHH FUUUCK!"

"Now now, not so loud."

"UUUGH!"

"Turn ya Bitch Ass over Ray-Ray."

"Do I know you?"

"You might, I'm responsible for Scraps and Jimmy's death."

"You Son of A." *(Pit, Pit)*

"Now, now next shot will be to tha head instead of tha arms."

"Do you remember Samad? Of course, you do, you killed him. Well, you may not know but he was my uncle and he wanted you to have this."

(PIT, PIT, PIT) **I HIT HIM 3 TIMES IN THE CHEST.**

"911 may I help you?"

"Yes, I heard gunshots at 411 Cresten Place."

"Yo, get outta here! Tha cops are on their way and keep ya mouth shut!"

"Naf."

"What up Cam?"

"Ya Boy is gonna be in ICU if he don't check out."

"My Boy who?"

"Ray-Ray."

"Cam what you talkin' bout?"

"I'll talk to you after I get dressed."

"Who's driving tonight?"

"I am but we all meeting up at tha crib."

"I'll be there in about an hour." All I could think about was what Cam had just said.

"Nafee is that you?"

"Who else is gonna be walking in here?"

"You home early."

"I came to get dressed."

"You going out?"

"Me, Cam and Trap going up top to 2 Dollar Tuesday."

"All you do is go out; you better have ya fun now cause once tha baby comes ya Ass gonna be helping out."

I put my clothes on the bed and then jumped in the shower. I could hear my phone repeatedly going off. I knew Shelly wouldn't answer it; not that any female except Toya would be calling.

"You sitting right there, I know you hear my phone going off."

"Do you answer my phone when it goes off and I'm not around?"

"Nah cause it's ya phone."

"Vice versa." I knew she would say that that's why I said it.

"I took tha liberty to pick you out a better outfit."

"Babe it's only 2 dollar Tuesday."

"OK and you said that to say what?"

It was an argument I knew I couldn't win so all I said was thank you. I rubbed her belly, kissed her on the forehead, told her I loved her, and then left.

"Nigga you worse than a broad we were about to leave you if it wasn't for her," Trap said pointing to Toya.

"You could have left, I know how to get there."

"Toya, I won't drive fast so you can keep up."

"I'm like Mario Andretti behind tha wheel; don't do me no favors."

"Just keep up."

"Trap turn that down; so, tell me what happened wit Ray-Ray?" After listening to what happen I was madder that he didn't kill him.

"Why did you let him live? Now he can identify you."

"He knows tha code of tha street."

"First thing in tha morning I'm going to find out his condition; if he's alive I'll do what you should've done."

"Killing him would be too good for him, I wanted him to suffer."

We'll deal wit it tomorrow; tonight, let's do what we do."

"Why is she flicking her lights?"

"Yo?"

"Tell that Nigga he drives like Nana."

"Yo, she said you drive like Nana."

"Oh, she got jokes," he said stepping on the gas.

"I wonder if she has any e-pills?"

"I got some she gave me," Cam said.

"You don't Fuck wit no e-pills."

"I did last time Toya was up here."

"No wonder you got my Cuz open." When we got to Transit, the line wasn't that long so we got right in.

"It's packed in here for a Tuesday."

"Let's get a drink."

"I want a double shot of Remy straight."

"Me too."

"I'll have a double-shot of Goose."

"You want an e-pill?" Toya whispered in my ear.

Even though I already had one I said, "Yes." Angel and Shonie could party just as good as Toya.

"Look at Cam, he just like you swear he can dance."

"I don't dance, I two step."

"Like Cassidy said, you got ya drink and ya two-step."

Around 10 o'clock a fight broke out and that was enough for me; I was ready to leave anyway.

"Naf you gonna ride back wit me since they riding wit them?"

"Do I have a choice?"

"No, now get ya Ass in!"

"Did you give them tha house key?"

"No why?"

"Just ask."

"I can't stay wit you tonight."

"I understand, I'm sure you will before I go home."

"I didn't say we couldn't get it in, I just can't stay."

"In that case, I better step on it." She got us to the crib in about 15 minutes.

"No talking, just get naked."

"I love a woman who takes control."

Two hours later, I was walking into my front door where Shelly was sleeping on the couch.

"Baby, Baby."

"Huh?"

"Come on get up, let's go to bed."

"I didn't even realize I fell asleep."

"Eeell slobber all on ya face, you must really be tired."

"I am."

"Come on, bedtime."

"Can we just sleep down here? I don't feel like getting up."

"Sure," I said taking my clothes off.

"This carpet is softer than our bed."

I had to agree with her. The carpet was so thick and soft, when we first moved in I use to sleep down here all the time. The way Shelly held on to me it was like she knew I was cheating. I did feel bad, but what was I to do?

When I woke up Shelly was gone, but she left a note saying her, Mil and Lil had gone to breakfast and she would call me later. I had a long day ahead of me so I got myself together.

"Christiana Hospital."

"Yes, I'm looking for a Raymond Upchild."

"Could you hold for a moment please?"

"Sure," a few minutes later she came back, "yes, he's in ICU."

"Is he allowed any visitors?"

"Immediate family only."

"What room is he in? I'm his brother."

"413."

"Thank you."

"You're welcome." Now that I knew what room he was in I had to move to phase two of my plan.

"Unh, unh, unh."

"What was that for?"

"Was it good?"

"Bitch that young boy got it going on like a Mafucka!"

"So does Trap."

"I know what though?"

"What?"

"I bet tha neighbors know his name if they didn't before."

"Bitch, you stupid," I said laughing.

"Why does he have to have a girl?"

"Listen to us, we're normally tha ones to have Mafucka's messed up."

"Toya, Trap had me in all positions I didn't even know existed."

"I guess we'll be in Delaware more often?"

"I know I will, wit or wit out yall."

"Shonie you hear this Bitch? She done had a good piece of Dick now she don't know how to act."

"Sooooo whaaat, it's been awhile since I had a good shot."

"It's been awhile since you had any." *(Ha! Ha! Ha!)*

"Only because I choose not to...Believe that!"

"We hit a soft spot."

"Just because you didn't get none don't hate."

"Never will I hate on my girls and for your info I did get me some of that goods last night."

"Excuse me."

"You're excused."

"So, ladies after you wash your asses, what's on the agenda."

"Well, since you tha only one who knows ya way around, we'll leave that up to you."

"I was thinking about going to Philly to do a little shopping."

"Now, you're speaking my language."

"Naf, I owe you big time for hooking me up wit Angel."

"It was that good huh?"

"They say birds of a feather flock together," Trap said with a smile.

"I need to call Shonie to see if she wants to go to Philly for tha day."

"Tha power of Pussy."

"I know you not talkin' Nigga tha way Toya got you open." Cam's phone started going off and the smile on his face said it all.

"Yo!"

"Hey Cam I was calling to let you know me, Shonie and Toya going to

Philly to do a little shopping."

"That's a coincidence; me and Trap were about to call and ask tha same thing, but if yall going wit Toya it's cool."

"I'm sure Toya can find something to do wit Naf; I'll be ready in an hour."

"Naf, we need you to find something to do wit Toya."

"I got something else to do that's really important."

"Well, you better include Toya."

"Toya, Cam and Trap wants to take us to Philly."

"Do you...I'll be cool, I'll hang out wit Naf."

"You sure?"

"Yes, go head."

"Shonie they said they'll be here in an hour."

"Then you better hurry up." While they hurried to get ready, I decided to call Naf.

"Hey you."

"Hey."

"You busy?"

"Not at tha moment; what's up?"

"Shonie and Angel just canceled our plans to go wit ya boys so I was hoping we could spend some time."

"A'ight, but there's something important that I need to handle first."

"Come get me, I'm sure I can be of some help."

"I don't want you to get involved in this."

"Now I definitely want in if you about to put some work in."

"I don't know why you smiling, I'm dead serious."

"How do you know I'm smiling?"

"Call it intuition."

"I'm on my way."

Trap and Cam were pulling off as I was pulling up.

"So, what's tha plan?"

"Ray-Ray was sent to ICU last night; I plan to finish tha job."

"Is his room guarded?"

"I don't know."

"Let's go to tha hospital first to see what's going on before we walked into there all gun ho."

"What room is he in?"

"413."

"Wait here, let me check it out first." Toya was definitely a ride or die chick hands down.

I made my way to the ICU, to my surprise there was no place anywhere. I slipped into the nurses' break room and broke into one of the lockers where there happened to be a pair of Scrubs. Once I put them on I stepped out.

"Janell, I need you to go to room 413 and checked his vitals. Janell, did you hear me?"

The doctor grabbed my arm, "Janelle did you hear me?"

Looking down at the name tag on my shirt I realized he was talking to me, "Oh yeah, I'm sorry I have a lot on my mind."

I put on a pair of surgical gloves before going into his room. Ray-Ray was laying there with tubes running through his body. Without any hesitation, I put the pillow over his face until all the life was out of his body. Just as I was about to go inside Toya when came back out.

"I thought you got lost in there."

"Nah, but let's get outta here."

"How many cops were in there."

"None."

"Well, I need to handle this now while I have tha chance."

"Just pull off, I took care of it," she said with a devilish smile.

"I don't know about you but I feel like doing a little shopping."

"Boy stop playing, you know that's my favorite 7 letter word."

"Don't you mean eight?"

"No spell it with one 'P' not two."

All I could do was laugh, "I need to make one stop first then we can roll."

"Do you, I'm on ya time." I stopped at one of my stash houses; grabbed some money and then headed to King of Prussia.

"I thought we were going shopping?"

"We are, King of Prussia."

"I heard that, say no more and turn this up."

SHE'S A GLAMOROUS GIRL AND SHE CAME TO ROCK MY WORLD ALL THE GUYS THAT WANNA GET WITH HER STEP BACK CAUSE YA KNOW YA CAN'T GET...

"Naf what you know about this?"

"My dad use to bump this."

“This is a classic right here.”

We splurged, everything on me. That was the least I could do; she had just killed a man for me, no questions asked. On the ride back, I couldn't help but wonder if this would trigger some feelings from Kev. Even though he didn't deal wit him that was still his blood.

“You a'ight? You look like you in deep thought over there.”

“Yeah, I'm cool; I was just thinking that's all.”

CHAPTER 26

Torn

"Hey Sis, you okay?"

"Of course, why wouldn't I be?"

"Considering ya son is in tha hospital fighting for his life."

"Kevin, I don't want to sound cruel, but I could care less if he dies."

"You don't mean that; you're just hurting right now."

"I stopped caring when my only son told me he wish I would just die."

"He said what?"

"You heard me."

"When did he say that?"

"About a month ago."

"How come you didn't tell me?"

"I didn't want to be tha cause of his death."

"God don't like ugly and Raymond was ugly, so he got what he deserved!"

"Kevin, can you answer that for me please?"

"Sure, hello...Yes she is hold on...It's tha hospital."

"Ask them what they want."

"She can't come to tha phone right now; can I take a message? Okay, I'll let her know. They said you need to come to tha hospital to sign some papers; Ray-Ray didn't make it." I needed to be here for her even though her mouth said she didn't care, her heart told a different story.

"Come on, I'll go wit you."

Now that Ray-Ray was out of the picture, we set up shop in the last two spots and business was booming on all levels. Between the yola and sour diesel the city was ours at all cost.

Shelly had my son, but was still on maternity leave trying to smother me like a blanket, which was pushing me into Toya's arms. Cam and Trap were in Atlanta so much they bought a crib down there.

"Hey you."

"What's up?"

"Just had you on my mind so I figured I give you a call."

"Toya I'm coming down for a few days; I need you to get away."

"You driving down by ya self?"

"I was thinking about flying down since Trap and Cam are already down there."

"Do you want me to book you a flight for tomorrow?"

"No, see if they have something available for tonight."

"Okay, I'll call you right back."

I felt bad that Naf was getting tired of Shelly, but I had fell in love with him over the past few months. Luckily, they had a flight that would be departing in the next few hours so I called Naf back to let him know.

"Just make sure you pick me up at tha airport."

"I'm on my way now."

"You funny, you know that?"

"Bye, I'll see you at tha airport."

"So, you going out of town?"

"Yeah, I'm going to see how to Trap and Cam is doing wit tha closing of tha lot."

"Who is she Naf?"

"What?"

"Tha Bitch you Fuckin; who is she?"

"Shelly don't start that dumb Shit again."

"Just don't let me find out cause Imma Fuck you and that Bitch up!" I didn't respond to that, I just went upstairs to pack my things.

"Make sure you stop by ya moms to see ya son before you go." I was doing that anyway since she was taking me to the airport.

"I gotta holla at Naf so we can let him know we plugged in down here."

"On some real Shit Trap, tha money on this end is better than up top so just imagine if we can expand down here."

TOYA WALKS IN

"Hey yall."

"Hey Toya."

"I talked to Naf a little while ago; he'll be down later tonight."

"He's driving by himself?"

"No he's flying in; I just have to pick him up from tha airport."

"That's what's up, I need to holla at him anyway."

"I'll holler at yall later."

"Cam it's something different about Toya, I just can't put my finger on it."

"Not to be disrespectful, but her Ass has gotten fatter."

"Maybe that's it."

"Between me and you, I think she might be knocked up."

"Nah, I don't think they having unprotected sex."

"Yeah, you probably right."

"Mom you ready?"

"Boy don't be rushing me, I'm coming.

"I got Lil Naf, we'll be in the car."

"Put him in ya truck."

"Okay."

On the way to the airport my mom asked me if I was cheating on Shelly. I never lied to my mom so I wasn't going to start now.

"Did Shelly tell you to ask me that?"

"No, but I sense tha change in you."

"Yeah, I got a friend."

"Naf, I know Shelly has been really smothering you and that's why you been doing you."

"I do love her mom, but she's been pushing me away."

"I know, I've seen it; you need to tell her how you feel."

"I do all tha time; it goes in one ear and out the other."

"Is this thing wit this other girl serious?"

"We've been talking for 6 months."

"So, that's where you're going now to visit her?"

"Yes, and to see how Trap and Cam are doing wit tha new shop."

"Oh, she's from Atlanta?"

"Yeah, its Traps cousin, and no he didn't hook us up."

"I wasn't going to ask; I just think you owe it to Shelly to tell her tha truth."

"I will when I get back."

"Now give me a kiss and go catch ya plane."

I looked at Lil Naf who had fallen asleep; I love you Lil Nigga.

"Naf."

"Yes."

"Decide what you wanna do before you get back."

"Mom, I'll be back in 2 weeks, love ya."

"Love you too Baby."

Before I boarded my plane, I called Ms. Barb from All Around Travel to book a 6 night 7 day all exclusive trip to the Virgin Islands scheduled to leave in two days. I slept for the flight to Atlanta, by the time I woke up the plane had landed.

"Hey Baby," Toya said hugging me tightly as if she hadn't seen me in months instead of two weeks. I returned her a hug with a soft but passionate kiss.

"Wow, you must of really missed me."

"You just don't know how much."

"Why don't you take me home and show me just how much you've missed me."

"No, I have an even better idea; the day after tomorrow we're going to tha Virgin Islands."

"Are you serious?" she asked all excited.

"Yup, for a week."

"Good, I have my yearly check-up tomorrow, so that works out perfect."

"Come on, let's get out of here."

"Cam said he needed to talk to you so make sure you call him."

"I'm going to call him once I get settled in."

"Well, I guess you won't be calling him tonight then," she said licking her lips seductively.

"Shelly why are you crying?"

"Naf is cheating on me."

"How do you know, do you have proof?"

"No, I just know he is; he's never home anymore."

"You know where he is when he's not home?"

"I told him Imma Fuck both of 'em up when I find out who she is."

"Shelly, you have to think about ya son; if he's cheating you don't need him."

"If it was Cam or Trap would you be saying the same thing?"

"I don't know about yall but if Cam was cheating on me I'd try to work it out first and if that doesn't work, I'll leave him."

"I'm not putting up wit that; Traps Ass would be history; end of story."

"Did you ask Ms. Cookie?"

"Yes, she said I need to ask him; she doesn't know."

"She probably wouldn't tell you anyway."

"She told me if he was cheating to kick his Ass to the curb."

"Ms. Cookie said that about her own son?"

"Yeah, she's a firm believer of one man, one woman; anything other than that they don't need to be together."

"I agree wit her on that."

"Why don't you just ask him?"

"I did and he denied it."

"But you don't believe him."

"Nope, I've been wit him too long to know when something's not right."

"Call Joey Greco. Ha! Ha! Ha!"

"I'm not calling no Damn Cheaters."

"Then leave it alone unless you have some proof."

I woke up the next morning to the smell of bacon, pancakes and eggs, but no Toya. There was a note taped to the microwave letting me know she went to the doctors. I ate, got dress, and then hit Cam's phone.

"What up Playboy?"

"I can't call it. What's good wit you?"

"We got Shit poppin' down here; that's what's up with us."

"What you talkin' bout?"

We bought some work down last time we came down and Toya turned us on to some folks who then turned some folk on.

"So, that's why you've been coming down so much."

"Yup, that and tha girls. We make about 10 Grand less, but we dump 30 in tha time we would dump 15."

"We losing 300g's"

"Not really, it's a quick flip so, in tha long run we making up for it."

"We can jump tha price up if you want another G."

"Nah, leave it; we might be able to fully expand. Plus, you know we put a quarter on every pie."

"If yall doing that then we good."

"They going crazy now, so imagine if we give it to 'em raw."

"Then you can charge tha extra 5 G's."

"I'm going away tomorrow for a week."

"You and Toya?"

"Yeah."

"Naf, what's tha deal wit you and Shelly?"

"Cam, she's pushing me away, Imma let her know about Toya when I get back."

"You not feeling good, maybe you need to lay down."

"I'm good, I just don't want to keep her in tha dark any longer she deserves to know."

"Aunt Cookie must've talked to you." All I could do was smile because he hit it on the nose.

"If that's what you really want to do I support you and I know Mil is gonna be on my heels once you do come clean."

"Where is Trap at?"

"He took Shonie to tha dentist."

"A'ight, I'll get wit yall later before I roll out."

"Hi you doing Latoya?"

"I couldn't be any better Dr. Hines."

"Well, everything is ok except that you're 8½ weeks pregnant."

"Pregnant!"

"Yes."

"I can't be, I've been still having my periods."

"That's normal, some people still do until they reach their 3rd month."

I didn't know whether to jump in the air or cry.

"You don't look too excited."

"I don't know how to feel right now. Where are they going?"

"Well, there are options you could consider, but I do want you to take a week to think about it and then come back to see me," she said handing me a card with a date for my next appointment.

On the ride home I was happy, but I didn't know if Naf would feel the same way or if he would think I was trying to trap him. I decided I would tell him tomorrow after we were in the Virgin Islands.

That night after I got out the shower, I looked at myself in the mirror. Was I ready to be somebody's mother? Was I ready to give up my carefree life? I knew I was stable, but was enough?

"You picked up some weight," Naf said smacking my Ass and startling me.

"Don't be sneaking up on me like that?"

I wanted to have a serious conversation with Toya, but decided to wait until tomorrow.

"You not hanging wit ya boys tonight?"

"Nope, just me and you; unless you want me to hang out?"

"You got jokes."

We watched movies until we both fell asleep. The alarm went off at 5 am. We had enough time to shower, get dressed, and grab a bite to eat before check-in time at the airport.

"Can you believe this is my first time leaving the country?"

"Yeah right, I know plenty of niggaz offered to take you away."

"Sure, they offered, but I declined. Naf, I'm not one of those anything broads; I can pay my own way."

"I'm sure you can, but who wouldn't want to save money sometimes?"

PASSENGERS PLEASE FASTEN YOUR SEATBELTS THE PLANE IS ABOUT TO TAKE OFF.

CHAPTER 27

The Virgin Islands

"Oh My God, tha water is so beautiful."

The plane landed just as smoothly as it took off. As soon as we got off the plane, this guy came up to us and said, "I got some good weed if you smoke."

"Let me see."

"Come pon de bathroom," he said.

"Babe, wait right here."

This dude pulled out the greenest weed I have ever seen. He didn't need to open it, I could smell it through the bag.

"How much?"

"How much ya want?"

"2 ounces."

"60 per ounce."

"A'ight," I said going into my pocket to retrieve the money, "if I run out, how can I reach you?"

"Ya got a number?"

"Yeah," I said giving him the number to the throwaway phone I had.

"No, no you take," he said giving me his number instead.

"I thought I was gonna have to come in and get you."

"Nah, we good, let's just head to tha hotel."

Once we checked in we made our way to our room which was huge.

"Damn! This like a mini apartment." I told Ms. Barb I wanted something real nice, but this was on another level.

"I'm bout to take a shower and change, it's hot."

"Well, I'm about to see if this is as good as it looks and smells. When you get out tha shower I need to talk to you."

"Okay, cause I need to do tha same."

"Wheeew! This some fire for real Damn."

"Baby what you yelling about?"

"This Shit here ain't no joke, I gotta take some of this back somehow. So, what did you wanna talk to me about?"

"You first," she said wit a look of nervousness on her face.

On my way to the airport, my mom asked me if I was cheating on Shelly. I thought Shelly told her to ask since that has been the topic in our household as of late. Like I told you, I never lie to my mom. So, I told her I was; she said that I owe it to Shelly to tell her the truth; so, when I get back I'm gonna tell her.

"Naf, I never ever wanted to come between tha two of you."

"I know that Toya; just like I never thought I would fall in love wit you, but I have."

"We fell for each other, it's nobody's fault. Naf, there's one more thing I need to tell you."

"Go ahead, I'm listening."

"I just found out I'm 8½ weeks pregnant and before you ask, it's yours."

"I wasn't going to ask."

"I'll understand if you don't want another child yet and I'm fully prepared to get an abortion."

"Whoa! First off, I don't believe in abortions. Secondly, whatever choice you make I support you; even if you don't want to keep it."

She didn't respond with words; only with a hug and tears rolling down her cheeks. Now not only did I have to tell Shelly about Toya, but another baby as well.

For the few days, Toya and I had a ball; especially on the nude beach. I think Toya was a little jealous how all the woman was staring, some even pointing at my penis.

"Come on, we better get off this beach before I catch a case."

"Yeah, me too," I said watching a few dudes check out her flawless body.

"Naf, I had a wonderful time this week."

"So, did I."

"I don't know what's gonna happen once you get back, but I've prepared myself for tha worst." I didn't answer; I just looked into her eyes and smiled kind of letting her know she was a'ight.

As soon as we got back to Toya's crib I passed out on the sofa. I heard the doorbell ring, but I was too tired and exhausted to even open my eyes.

"Damn Bitch you got black."

"I know, now she looks like a Dominican."

"Ha! Ha! Ha! Yall crazy."

"So, how was it?"

"I had a ball; come on let's go into tha kitchen so we don't wake Naf."

"You must of put ya thing down, that Nigga out like a light."

"Shonie we had so much fun."

"That's what's up, I'm glad to see you happy again you deserve it."

"I didn't get to tell yall before I left, but I'm pregnant." They both jumped up screaming causing Naf to run in the kitchen.

"Sssh, keep it down, yall gonna wake my Baby."

"Too late for that," he said standing in the doorway.

"I'm sorry Baby."

"Congrats, Angel said, 'I guess our kids will be cousins."

"Bitch you lying."

"I just found out I'm 6 weeks today."

"Have you told Cam yet?"

"No, so don't run ya mouth."

"It's not my place to tell him."

"I called him, but he was taking care of something; he said he would down tomorrow."

"Toya, I'm going upstairs, please don't wake me up for nobody."

"A'ight."

"Both yall Bitches knocked up, unh, unh, unh."

"You next."

"No I'm not, we have protected sex."

"So do me and Naf."

"I see."

"Nah, one-time tha condom broke and it was feeling to Damn good to stop."

"Well, me and Cam never wear condoms, so I knew it was only a matter of time."

"You was trying to get knocked up?"

"Not really."

"Yeah, what ever, tell that to somebody who don't know no better or might even believe it."

"Fuck you Shonie!"

"Toya did yall try the nude beach out?"

"Yeah, I thought I was going to catch a case."

"Why?"

"All these broads kept looking at Naf's Shit while they were wit their man."

"Are you serious?"

"Dead serious, I don't blame them though, he hung like a horse."

"Must run in tha family."

"You mean friendship." We all started laughing and daping each other.

"I'm telling you, we all need to go somewhere together."

"I know."

"Oh yeah, you know Naf is telling his girl about me when he goes home."

"You got that Good Good for real."

"His mom told him he needs to tell her."

CHAPTER 28

The Truth

"Hey, how was ya trip?"

"It was fun, I had time to put a lot into perspective; Mom Toya is 3 months pregnant."

"You must really like this girl to have unprotected sex."

"The condom broke."

"Is tha baby yours?"

"Yes, she's not like that Mom."

"Well, when do you plan to tell Shelly?"

"As soon as I get home." Little did I know I was in for a Hell of a surprise.

"I told her you wouldn't be home til Thursday."

"It's cool, I'll surprise her."

"I have to pick up my grandson and then I'll bring him home later, that way yall can have some time to talk."

I pulled up in the driveway to find Shelly's car and another car that looks familiar, but I couldn't remember from where. I opened the door, but nobody was downstairs. I could hear voices coming from upstairs so I made my way up the steps. When I got closer, I thought the sounds my ears heard were the TV until I peeked through and saw Shelly on her back with her legs in the air. At that point, I was full of rage.

"You Bitch!" Shelly pushed the dude off her.

"What tha Fuck, ya cousin? You're a sick Bitch!"

"I can explain!"

"No need! I want you out of my house," I said going to the closet taking all of her Shit out, "and you," I said walking towards Josh, "you been smiling in my face for years!"

"Nigga I don't owe you Shit!"

"So, how long yall been Fuckin?"

"Just as long as you."

"Well, you can have this Whore."

"Fuck you Nafee ya mom is a Whore."

"Bitch if you ever disrespect my mom I will stomp a mud in ya Dumbass."

"Nigga, you ain't gonna do Shit," Josh said stepping in front of her.

"Ya best bet is to quit while you're ahead."

"You Little Punk Ass Nigga," he said taking a swing at me.

I sidestepped it and followed up with my own combo knocking him down. When I was about to finish him off Shelly got in front of him.

"Leave him alone."

"Bitch get out of my house and I'll see you in court."

"For what? LJ is not your son."

"LJ?"

"Yes, that's my son's name; check his birth certificate if you don't believe me." I really lost it and pulled my gun out.

"Bitch you got 2 minutes to get you and ya Punk Ass Babies Daddy up outta my house!" As soon as they left I called my mom.

"Hey Baby, I'm on my way to get Little Naf."

"Mom you better not pick him up and I mean it."

"Naf what's tha matter, is everything a'ight?" I explained everything that had just went down and how Shelly told me that my son wasn't really my son.

"Meet me at tha house."

"I'll be there as soon as tha locksmith gets here." On my way to my mom's Toya called.

"Hey you."

"Hey."

"Why you sound like that, is everything okay?"

"Yeah, you don't have to worry about Shelly. I just walked in on her Fucking this nigga that she said was her cousin for tha last 6 years."

"Oh my, I'm sorry to hear that."

"Don't be, she did us a favor."

"Well, as long as you take care of Little Naf that's all that matters."

"Oh, I forgot to mention, that's not my son."

"What?

"Yeah, she said that his name is LJ; she named him after his real dad."

"How could she do that?"

"I guess what goes around comes around."

"All you did was give it back to her for all tha years' she was doing it to you."

"Yeah, if you look at it like that, I guess you right. I just can't believe she played me like that wit my son, I mean that baby. I did tell my mom he didn't look like me. It hurts but I'm glad I found out now while he was only a few months instead of years' so it won't be that hard to detach myself from him.”

“Naf I know you’re hurt and I don’t want you to think that I’m like Shelly so we can get a blood test in a few months if you want.”

“Toya, I know you wouldn’t do that; you have already proven ya loyalty. I just pulled up to my mom; I’ll call you in a little while.”

“Make sure you call me.”

“Stop playing, you know I am.”

“Naf.”

“Yo.”

“Just in case you need to hear it, I love you.”

“That’s what’s up.”

My mom was standing in the door by the time I got out of my truck.

“Hey, you okay?” my mom asked giving me a hug.

“Yeah, I’m fine.”

“I called Porsha, she said she didn’t know what I was talking about and she would call me back once she talked to Shelly.” My mom’s phone went off; she had a pissed look when she answered so I knew it was Shelly.

“Hello.”

“Ms. Cookie I just wanted to apologize.”

“For calling me a whore?”

“The whole situation, I really did love Nafee.”

“Listen Shelly, I love my son more than life itself.”

“I know you do.”

“Then when I say we have nothing to talk about you should understand

and not call my phone anymore." My mom didn't give her a chance to respond before hanging up.

"Mom you don't have to stop dealing wit her because of me."

She looked at me straight in the eyes and then said, "Nafee you're my only child, I will move mountains for you not to mention my grandson that I loved and cherished isn't even my grandson." When I saw my mom crying it tore me apart.

"Mom it's a'ight, you lost a grandchild but you gained another one."

"Nafee are you sure this is your child?"

"With out a doubt. She even said we could get a DNA in a few months if I wanted to be certain considering what I just went through."

"That's a good idea."

"Mom, I trust her with my life."

"Wow, you must really love her to say that; I need to meet her."

"I think she's coming up in a few days; let me call and ask her."

"Hey you."

"Hey, I was calling to see when you was coming up here."

"I don't know, why?"

"My mom wants to meet you."

"Ya mom?"

"Yeah, my mom Thurl."

"I sure am, let me see that phone...Hello."

"Hello."

"Hi, I'm Cookie, Nafees mother. Yes, I do want to meet tha woman who has my son saying he trusts you with his life and tha mother of my future grandchild."

"Ms. Cookie I'll be up there no later than Saturday."

"Well, I'll be expecting to see you; too bad you pregnant or we could hit the club together."

"We can, I'm not showing yet. Naf said once I start showing it's over."

"Well, Doc B is having a party Saturday."

"Tha last one me and my girls came up for was off tha chain, so I'll be up Thursday or Friday."

"I'll see you then. Nafee come get tha phone."

"Yo."

"Ya mom sounds cooler than a fan."

"She is, you'll love her."

"She invited me to go to Doc B's party wit her."

"Oh, she did?"

"Yup, so I'll be up by Thursday."

"That's tha day after tomorrow."

"I know when it is."

"I'll book 3 First Class tickets."

"Unh, unh I wanna drive up."

"I'll get you a rental did when you get here."

"Naf, I'm driving and that's all it is."

After I left my moms I went by the shop to catch up on some paperwork and have my truck detailed. Cam and Trap were out front when I pulled up.

"Yo, what's tha deal Playboy, you cool?"

"I'm straight, Fuck that Bitch!"

"What Bitch?"

"Mil and Lil didn't tell yall?"

"Tell us what?"

"I walked in on Shelly and Josh Fuckin."

"Say word."

"Nigga you lying, that's her cousin."

"We thought he was. That Bitch was playing me like a violin all these years."

"Word."

"That's not tha best part."

"Damn, there's more?"

"Yeah, Lil Naf ain't mines, his name is LJ."

"You gotta be lying."

"Do I look like I'm lying?"

"Yo that Bitch ain't Shit. What did Aunt Cookie say?"

"She snapped and cursed Shelly out when she hit her phone."

"Yo, I can't believe her. I wonder if Mil is cheating?"

"Tha thing is I'm not mad cause I was doing me, but for that not to be my son. Also, I'm going to get checked out to make sure I don't got Shit."

"I definitely feel you on that."

"You know that Nigga had tha nerve to swing on me."

"No."

"Yes, he did and I sat him on his Ass then this Bitch jumps in front of him so I couldn't stump him out."

"I would have stomped her Ass too."

"I just pulled my Shit out and made them both get out."

"She got tha nerve to come here." I turned around to see Shelly pulling up wit Mil and Lil in the car.

"We need to talk."

"I said what I had to say."

"I need my stuff and you change tha locks."

"What stuff?"

"My clothes."

"I paid for all that Shit, besides I gave it to Goodwill."

"Mafucka!" she said coming at me. Cam stepped in front of me, "no move Cam! Imma cut his Ass up!"

"Shelly Imma ask you nicely to leave before I call tha cops."

"I bet you would you; Police Ass Nigga."

"Tell ya cousin to buy you some clothes, I mean your man, baby daddy, whatever he is to you."

"He gonna kick ya Ass when he sees you."

"We tried that remember? You had to save his Ass."

"I'll call him now."

"Please don't do that for his safety. Matter fact, you do need to call him for a ride cause you're not driving my car."

"Mafucka, you wish it was ya car."

"It is, I never switched it in ya name."

"I bet I leave in it. Come on yall."

"Lil and Mil, I have nothing against yall, but don't get in there; I'm going to report it stolen."

"You ain't Shit Bastard."

"You did this. You should have just been woman enough to say you wanted out."

"Nigga you was doing you anyway."

"I was actually coming home to let you know that it was time for us to move on; we grew apart." She opened her phone to call Josh, so I thought.

"Hello."

"Yes, I've just been assaulted; yes, he's still here," she said giving them the address to the shop, "we'll see who gets tha last laugh now."

"Shelly that's Bullshit and I'm not going to let you get my brother locked up."

"Too bad. My girls seen him slap me, right yall?" Both Mil and Lil look at all of us like what do we do.

"Well, you better not lie for this Bitch," said Cam.

"Ya mom's a Bitch!" Cam went to grab her, but Mil stepped in his way.

"Baby don't do it."

"I'm not. Naf I'll stomp ya Dumb Ass out and ya Punk Ass Nigga. Now try me! Oh, did you just put ya hands on me too?"

"Unh, unh Shelly, you not doing that Shit to Cam."

"She's not doing it to Naf either; Lil you better not lie for her," Trap said in a serious tone.

"You can't tell her what to do."

"Shelly don't put me in tha middle of yall Shit." When the police arrived Shelly really put on a show.

"Can somebody tell me what happened?"

"Yes officer, I came to bring my friends to see their boyfriends when he started cursing me out for no reason."

"Then what happened?"

"I told him I didn't want to be wit him no more that's when he smacked me."

"Officer she's lying. I put her out of my house and she came to ask for her clothes. I told her I gave them to Goodwill and she threatened to cut me. Then I told her she needed to find another ride home because I was taking my car back and if she drove away I would report it stolen; that's when she called 911."

"Were all of you here?"

"Yes."

"Is that what happened?"

Cam and Trap said, "Yes."

"Ladies?" They both looked at Shelly then Mil and said yes but Lil said she was in the bathroom.

"Well, I'm going to have to place you under arrest, you guys can sort it out in court."

"Cam call Marc and my mom. Officer please don't let her leave in my car."

"It's not his, he gave it to me."

"Let me run the tags to see who it comes back to. Sorry Miss but the car comes back to a Nafee Jackson."

"That's me."

"I know but I'm going to have to take you to the station."

"I understand. Trap put a 'For Sale' sign on the window and leave it in the lot."

"Yo you selling it? How much you want?" one of the workers asked.

"5 Grand wit everything."

"I'll take it."

"You gonna need it for bail!" Shelly yelled with a big smile on her face.

"Shelly, you know that ain't right."

"Fuck you! Mil you pose to be my girl and you riding wit that Nigga over me?"

"I'm not going to send him to jail for something I know he didn't do."

"Why tha Fuck didn't you tell tha truth?" Trap asked Lil."

"I didn't want to get involved."

"Fuck that Shit, you might as well have said he did it."

"Next time I will then."

"You know what? You two deserve to be friends; lose my number. I'm done wit you. As far as I'm concerned this has been over for a few months now; I gotta friend anyway."

"I know you do, ain't nothing slow about me but the way I walk and make love."

"You wanna come clean to Cam?" Mil asked.

"I have nothing to come clean about."

"Josh, I need you to come pick me up from Naf's shop. Just come get me, I'll explain it to you when you get here."

After they finished processing me I got to use the phone. I called my mom who was waiting on my call.

"Have you gotten bail yet?"

"No, I haven't seen a judge yet."

"Me and Marc are out front waiting."

JACKSON TIME TO SEE THE JUDGE

"I gotta see tha judge now, I'll call you as soon as I'm done."

"Nafee Jackson Ya Honor."

"Mr. Jackson you're charged with Assault 2nd against a Shelly Brown."

"Ya Honor, that's my ex-girlfriend; I broke up wit her yesterday and put her out. She came to my place of buz-ness threatening and cursing me out when I told her to call a ride because she wasn't driving my car and she called 911."

"Well, seeing that you've never been in trouble before I'm going to set bail at 5,000 unsecured."

"So, I have to pay 5,000 to get out?"

"No, all you have to do is sign some papers and you're free to go. You'll get something in the mail telling you when to come to court."

"Officer can I use tha phone?"

"No sign here, here, and here; then you're free to go."

My mom and Marc were parked out front when I walked outside.

"Baby you a'ight?"

"Yes Mom, I'm fine."

"I called Porsha she said that she would make Shelly drop tha charges."

"She don't have to do that, I'll beat these wit my eyes closed."

"Why she do this? You caught her cheating."

"I took her car from her and sold it to somebody at tha shop right in front of her."

"You wild Naf."

"If Toya wasn't pregnant I'd get her to beat tha Shit outta her," he said.

"Speaking of Toya, she called my phone."

"How did she get ya number?"

"Cam, she was pissed. She said that she was on her way but I think she was just upset."

"Nah Ma, she's on her way."

"No, she's not."

"Watch this," I called Toya.

"Hello."

"Hey you."

"Are you Ok? I was worried."

"Yeah Shelly just on some petty Shit, nothing major."

"Not this time anyway."

"Where you at in tha house?"

"Hell no, I'm coming through North Carolina."

I looked at my mom and then said, "I told you."

"Told me what?"

"My mom didn't think you was really on ya way, but I told her you were."

"You Damn right! I'm going to stop to this before it gets out of hand." I knew she meant sending Shelly to the boneyard.

"Toya there's other ways of dealing withl this," I told her taking the phone off speaker so she would wouldn't say something crazy.

"Listen Naf, I know you probably still have feelings for her, but it is evident that she does not feel tha same way because if she did she would've never have called the police."

"Toya, let me be clear on one thing, I don't play that cop Shit. So, once she called, any feelings I may have had left, were gone."

"If she sees that she can get away wit it once, no telling what she might do next time."

"I feel what you saying."

"Cam said she came at you wit a box cutter."

"She did, but even if he didn't step in tha way I would've never let her cut me."

"Well, I'll be up there in a few hours."

"A'ight, is Shonie and Angel wit you?"

"Of course."

"Okay, slow down and call me when you get close."

"Boy that girl must really love you to be on her way up here."

"What's not to love about me, I am my mother's son."

"You sure are."

CHAPTER 29

Suicide

"Hey Mom."

"I'm in tha kitchen. Did Toya get here yet?" she said before turning around.

"Yes, I'm here Miss Cookie."

My mom turned around and said, "Wow you're pretty."

"I know you didn't think she was ugly."

"No but I had no ideal she was this beautiful either."

"Now you got me blushing."

"You could pass for Naf's sister."

"People say that all tha time, I know I look younger than my 35 years."

"I hope I look that good when I get that age."

"How old are you now, 20?"

"I wish, try 23."

"Chile, you gonna probably look even better if you're 23 now."

"I hope so, I want to be a thurl mom to my son or daughter."

"At least we know his or her grandmother will be." We all laughed at that.

"Toya, I don't want you to worry about Shelly, you don't need that kind of stress."

"I'm not worried about her, but she's not going to put Naf through all this bull either."

"Trust me, she's not."

"I love my son to death and I refuse to let anyone harm him or put him in a position where he could possibly end up in jail."

"We feel tha same way Ms. Cookie."

"I know that we have only been messing for 7 months, but we have a strong connection that I can't even explain."

"Baby sometimes when two people are so much alike they just click. Like me and his dad, God rest his soul. I hope yall hungry, I made enough for yall."

"I see, I thought you were having a party wit all this food."

"Boy shut up, this ain't no lot of food. Toya where are your friends?"

"Wit Cam and Trap."

"Yall are a mess."

"Dad had a side thing," I said joking.

"I didn't have to worry about that, ya dad respected me too much to hurt me, not to mention it wouldn't be worth losing me for a night of unmeaningful sex."

"Cam has a baby on tha way."

"How you know?"

"Nevermind, Aunt Jonda told you. He needs to tell that girl he wit."

"That's his biz-ness not ours."

"Naf, you know Trap told Shonie it's over between him and that other girl cause she lied to tha police instead of just telling tha truth."

Once we were done eating we went back to my house so I could get the rest of Shelly's stuff and drop it at her mom's house.

"This is really a nice house."

"I'm moving and putting it on tha market."

"What are you doing wit her stuff?"

"Taking it to her mom's house."

"I'm riding wit you."

"I know you are, come on."

Ms. Porsha was on the porch with the baby when we pulled up.

"You need my help?"

"No just sit there, it won't take long."

"How you doing Naf?"

"I'm fine and you?"

"I'm fine."

"Hey Lil Man." As I was unloading the last box Josh and Shelly pulled up.

"I know you didn't have tha nerve to bring no Bitch over to my mom's house." I didn't answer I just put the last box on the porch.

"I'll see you later Ms. Porsha."

"OK Naf."

"Fuck him and that Bitch." By now Toya was out of the car.

"Excuse me but I did not direspect you so please don't disrespect me."

"Bitch you better get ya Ass back in that truck before you catch a serious beat down." I grabbed Toya by her arm but she snatched away.

"You right, Imma get my Ass back in tha truck only because I don't wanna disrespect ya mom or ya child."

"No, you gonna get in there cause you don't want no beat down Bitch."

Toya tried to be the bigger woman by walking away but Shelly pushed her from behind causing her to fall into the truck. Before I could say anything, Josh had a pistol pointed at me.

"Now try to be a hero and give me a reason to squeeze."

I had left my gun in the truck so I wasn't in a position to say Shit.

Toya got up and said, "Remember you did this to ya self." Before Shelly knew what hit her Toya threw a 1-2-1 combo that sat her on her Ass.

"Unh, unh yall break that up!" Ms. Porsha yelled.

Josh helped Shelly up who was kicking and screaming for him to let her go.

"Shelly, you better calm ya Ass down, I'm not gonna have that around my house."

"You better listen to ya mom before this Shit get messy," Toya said still in her fighter stance.

"Bitch you got that one, Imma see you again."

"You should just take ya lose and more on."

"She's not going to be fighting not while she's carrying my child."

That statement sent Shelly over the edge.

"Bitch Imma Fuck you up."

Josh grabbed Shelly's arm, "Calm ya Ass down!"

"Come on let's go." I made a mental note to get with Corey about Josh.

"It's probably not ya baby anyway."

I could tell that Shelly was still in love with Naf just by the way she was acting.

"Damn Toya a 1-2-1 combo. How long you been boxing?"

"Who said I know how to box?"

"I know a little something about boxing."

"My step pop taught me when I was younger. He always said I was going to be gorgeous when I got older and a lot of females would want to fight me because of that. Was he right?"

"He sure was. Next time extend ya arm on tha jabs with more power."

"Like you really know."

"I've been boxing close to 11 years."

"Well, I guess we'll be training for tha next 6 months."

"I train every morning for 2 hours."

"I plan to stay in shape while I'm pregnant. I need to maintain this lovely figure," she said running her hands over her body.

"I knew she would be calling...Hello."

"Boy what is going on? Porsha just called me talking all stupid." I explained the whole situation to her play by play.

"She kicked Shelly's Ass, huh?"

"Mom, I knew Toya was vicious, but I had no idea she was nice wit her hands like that."

"Don't be fooled by her pretty face. Shelly also called to say that she was going to beat her baby out of her. I already let her know that she'll be in W.C.I. faster than she can say I'm sorry."

"Mom, she needs to just move on like I have."

"Nafee, she knows she messed up and it's killing her on tha inside."

"I'll stop by tomorrow when you get off work."

"OK. And Nafee, stay outta trouble please."

"I always do Mom, love ya."

"You too."

"Naf I'm telling you now that Bitch is treading on thin ice. If she likes breathing, she better leave me tha Fuck alone."

"She's miserable so she wants everybody else to be."

"Yeah, but she did that to herself."

"I know...Hold up for a sec, I need to make a call."

"Don't."

"Huh?"

"Don't make that call to have Homeboy killed."

"Why not?"

"Simple. Not saying that you can't trust whoever you were going to call because I'll sure you can or you wouldn't be calling him."

"But why give somebody an ace card later down tha line if they ever need one."

"If it's not Trap or Cam don't make that call."

"Well, what do you suggest I do?"

"I suggest we handle it."

"Noooo, you not getting involved."

"Listen. Pussy is every niggaz weakness.

"He just seen you kick his girl's Ass, so I doubt he'll go for that."

"You're probably right, but he's never seen Shonie or Angel."

"If I don't give one person a trump card. Why would I give two?"

"To set tha record straight, my girls are just like me."

"Question. When you say just like you, what do you mean?"

"I think you know what I mean."

"Let me find out some info and I'll get back wit you."

"Don't take to long."

Naf still hadn't got back with me and tonight was the night of Doc B's party.

"Toya, you think this dude gonna come to tha party tonight?"

"I'm sure all tha ballers will be in tha building tonight."

"If I was still on my Bullshit, I would be excited."

"So, let's go over tha plan one last time."

"No need, it's simple. You see him, point him out and I'll handle tha rest."

"Trap said I better not even let him kiss me."

"We better get ready."

Two hours later, we were all dressed and sitting in Ms. Cookie's living room waiting on her.

"Mom! Mom!"

"Boy if you don't stop all that Damn yelling."

"They're down here waiting on you."

"Here I come now," she said coming down the steps.

"DAAAAMN! Aunt Cookie, you looking realy fly!"

"Where is ya mom at?"

"Right here."

"Wow! Yall trying to show them young girls off tonight," said Trap.

"Trap you know my mom and aunt stay fly."

"I know but tonight they along wit Toya, Shonie, and Angel setting tha bar extremely high."

"Way to clean it up," Shonie said punching him in the arm.

I couldn't front, the 5 of them definitely was looking good.

"Come on yall we out! Naf, I'm driving ya truck so we don't have to drive two cars."

"I'm riding wit them anyway, so we'll see yall later on."

"Cookie look at this long ass line."

"Since when have we ever waited in line at any club?"

"You ain't never lied about that." We parked and then walked to the front of the line where they had a separate line for VIP.

The man at the door said, "It's $75 for ladies to get in this line."

"You said that like we don't got it."

"Nah, I was just letting yall know in case you didn't"

"Well, we do plus some," Ms. Jonda let him know.

"No need to get hostle, mayble I can T-pain you."

"Nah, maybe you can buy one of those chicken heads a drink. I pay my own way."

"Is there a problem up here?"

"Nah, ain't no problem."

"Who dis ya man?" he asked.

"Nah nigga, her son."

"Ya son?"

"Yeah, her son."

"Wow, you sure don't look that old."

"Because I'm not. Now if you'll excuse us." He stepped to the side to let them pass.

"No disrespect Peeps. I was just trying to buy her a drink."

"She's grown, I was just making sure she was good."

"Nigga is you gonna stay out here and talk to him all night or we going in?"

We paid once we got through the door.

"You know tha dumb ass broad gonna be here tonight."

"I know but she won't try nothing wit my mom here."

"I told Mil to stay her Ass home."

"She probably didn't care, it aint like she goes out that much anyway."

I FUCKED MY MONEY UP, DAMN NOW I CAN'T RE-UP RAN OFF IN HIS SPOT JUST TO GET MY STACKS UP NOW I'M BACK ON DECK.

"This that Shit right here!"

"This that Waka Floka Nigga?"

"Yeah."

"Look at that Sucka Ass Nigga falling for tha bait."

"I don't want no smoke wit ya peeps my girl told me she be trippin."

"If you had something like this, wouldn't you?"

"I sure would."

"What you doing after this?"

"It depends on what you wanna do."

"Here, take my number. Call me when you leave."

"Don't be playing no games."

"Nah Ma, I'm definitely trying to see you bout something."

"Just answer tha phone," I said walking away making my Ass bounce just cause I knew he was watching.

"Damn, Imma hit that after this."

"Shelly not having that."

"Nigga Imma dip on her. I'm not passing that Shit up."

"Let's hit tha bar up."

"Trap what tha biz-ness?"

I turned around to see who was talking to me. *This nigga got a lot of nerve," I thought to myself,* "I can't call it."

"Let me buy you a drink," he said pulling out a knot of money.

"I already paid for a bottle of Ace of Spade."

"I got you. How much is it?"

"300."

"That's all?"

"Yeah."

He peeled off 4 one hundred dollar bills. I wanted to smack the Shit out of him for tying to disrespect me, but instead I told everybody at the bar that drinks were on me and for the bartender to keep the change.

Shelly and Lil walked up to Josh and his man.

"Hey Boo," she said loud enough for Naf to hear.

"Damn you look Sexy Ass a Mafucka."

"Yo yall lets go take a few pictures."

"Come on, but let's find Aunt Cookie and my mom."

"No need, they just found us."

"Hey we came to see if yall wanted to take some pictures wit ya moms."

"We were on our way to ask yall tha same thing."

"Hey Ms. Cookie, Ms. Jonda."

"Hello Shelly." I just smiled and grabbed Toya's hand and let her to the picture booth.

Josh and his boys came up next to us. When he stepped on my foot, I knew it wasn't no accident, but I didn't say Shit. I just smiled, wiped my shoe off, and kept talking to Toya.

A few minitues later, Shelly came out talking loud, just wanting to be seen or heard.

"If if ain't tha get along gang." When nobody responded, she repeated herself.

"Look ain't nobody for that Shit tonight Shelly so fall back!" Cam said.

"Fuck you Cam! Get a Life!"

"Shelly, you need to calm down and enjoy ya self tonight."

"I'm trying to, but it's just so much hate in tha air."

"All coming from you."

"Cam don't start it wit her," my mom said.

"Mom that's her."

"What did I say?"

"Still getting scolded by mom…Awe that's so cute," Shelly said sarcastically. I didn't say Shit, I just ice grilled Josh's Punk Ass. We partied for another hour before we decided to break out.

"Hello."

"I didn't think you was gonna call."

"I wanted to make sure you had everything in order before I did."

"You need me to come pick you up?"

"Nah, I can meet you somewhere."

"Do you know where tha Red Roof Inn is in Newark?"

"Yeah."

"Meet me there."

"A'ight, I'll call you when I get close."

"Yall ready to do this?"

"Yeah, we'll follow you."

"Shonie don't let that Nigga touch you."

"Baby I may have to let him feel a little Ass or Tits."

"We better get going before he starts blowing my phone up."

"Hey, I'm pulling into tha parking lot now."

"I'm in Room 313."

"Give me 10 minutes then come in, he'll be naked by then if he's not already." When I got to the room the door was slightly open so I walked in.

"You don't waste no time, do you?"

"No need to, we both know why we came."

"You're right about that." I saw his gun in the chair under his shirt so I eased over to remove it with out him noticing.

"You gotta let me put this blind fold on you."

"Oh, you one of those freaky Bitches."

"You better watch ya Fuckin Mouth Nigga."

"My bag, no need to get uptight."

"Put tha blind fold on me." Cam, Naf, and Trap walked in with guns drawn.

"Damn Ma, what's taking so long? Let's get this show started."

"Since you insist." Josh snatched the blind fold off at the sound of Naf's voice.

"What tha Fuck is this!?"

"You didn't think I was going to let you get away wit pulling that gun on me now did you?" He went for his gun.

"Looking for this?" Shonie asked pointed his gun at him.

"You Bitch!"

"Is that anyway to talk to tha woman that was about to give you tha best Fuck of your life?"

"Trap give him tha pen and paper." None of us knew why he wanted us to bring a pen and paper so we were eager to find out.

"If you want to live a little longer you'll write everything I tell you to. Now let's start wit I am writing this letter because I can no longer go on living my life like this.

"What tha Fuck!?"

"Sssh no talking, just write. Now, where were we? Oh yeah, I feel it's time for me to come clean about who I really am and that's a homosexual."

"Man, you tha Fuck crazy! I'm not writing no Shit like that!!"

"Well fine. Who wants to kill him?" Trap and Cam both pointed their guns at him.

"Hold up! Hold up!"

"You have a change of heart? Now since we got that out tha way. Too many people have suffered behind this so I can no longer live. Wipe his gun down and everything in this room you touched. Are you left or right handed?"

"Left," he said lying.

"Put tha gun in his right hand," I said handing Shonie the gun I had.

As soon as she put the pistol in his hand she moved it to his head.

(PIT)

"Come on and leave tha pistol in his hand." Trap left with Shonie while Cam and I left together.

"Aye yo, that was some clever Shit if I do say so myself."

"I don't need nothing to come back to me."

"I gotta meet wit Uncle Kev first thing in tha A.M."

"Cam, we have another problem that needs to be addressed."

"Whats that?"

"I think we have a rat in our circle."

"What makes you say that?"

"Mr. Willy said tha police booked him for taking a piss outside and while he was locked up he overheard tha police questioning somebody about our operation."

"OK and?"

"And they were telling what they knew."

"We don't do no hand to hand so we cool."

"Yeah, but we got people who do."

"Mr. Willy didn't get a chance to see his face or catch his name?"

"He saw his face, but he doesn't know him so we gonna ride thru tha city and see if he can spot 'em."

"Damn! Who Can U Trust?"

CHAPTER 30

Traitor

The news spread like a wild forest fire about Josh killing himself and coming out the closet. Shelly took it hard and Ms. Porsha made her get tested.

"Nafee did you go get that test done?"

"Of course, I did and if that Bitch gave me that Shit I swear on my pops Imma kill her."

"You won't have to worry about that, I promise you."

I had heard that my mom was about her business. For Shelly's sake, she better hope my baby doesn't have HIV.

"Mom, are you cooking tonight?"

"I wasn't. Marc invited me to dinner."

"Yall pretty serious?"

"He's good to me."

"As long as you're happy. That's all that matters to me."

"I am."

"I'll call you later mom."

"A'ight…When is Toya coming back up?"

"I don't know, but I'm going down there next week."

CAM AND MR. WILLY IS IN SEARCH OF THE SNITCH

"Oh Shit! Cam that's him right there."

"Which one?"

"Tha one in tha blue Yankees fitted."

"You sure?"

"Positive."

"I knew that Nigga couldn't be trusted! I knew it!"

"You know him?"

"Very well. Mr. Willy now you sure that's tha nigga you seen?"

"Cam, I'm as sure as tha sky is blue."

"Say no more then. I need to call Naf and Trap."

"Drop me back in tha trap."

"I got you." After I dropped Mr. Willy off, I made my way to the shop to meet up with Naf and Trap.

"There's something in your eyes Babe that's telling me you want me Girl."

"Hello."

"Were you busy?"

"Nah, on my way to tha shop. How you feeling?"

"I'm okay once I get past tha morning sickness."

"I'll be down there next week wit Naf."

"Good cause I miss you."

"Ya mom emailed me."

"I know, she told me she did. She's just so excited to become a grandmom. She's driving me crazy."

"My mom is doing tha samething to me."

"I'll call you later, Toya is here to pick me up for lunch."

"A'ight, tell her I said hi."

The shop was packed as usual. I told Naf for the summer time we needed to have broads in bikini's washing the cars.

"What's up Fellas" I went in the shop to order me some curly fries and fingers.

"Ya Girl cameby to get her car cleaned earlier."

"Shit, I forgot I was suppose to get it done for her."

"Yeah, she said that but she wasn't mad."

"Call me when mt food is finished. I'll be in tha back."

"I'll have Cindy bring it to you."

"That works for me. Trap, Naf, whats up?"

"I thought I saw ya truck out there."

"Yeah, I had to order something to eat. I'm hungry as a Mafucka."

"So, what was so important?"

"Me and Mr. Willy were riding around and he spotted tha nigga who was doing tha talking."

"Who was it?" When I told them both of their faces went blank.

"Was he sure it was him?"

"That's tha samething I asked him and he assured me that it was wit out a doubt."

"Damn, I never thought in a million years' he would cross over."

"I hate to be tha one to say it but…I told you so."

"If only I would have listened, we wouldn't be having this conversation right now."

"You can't blame ya self; you did what either of us would have done."

"That still does not change tha fact he's a rat no matter what it's always death before dishonor!"

"Ain't no telling what he's already told them or how long he's been working wit them."

"About 3 months."

"What you talking bout Cam?"

"Remember when he said he was robbed for a half brick?"

"Yeah, and you thought he was lying."

"He was that Nigga that got booked wit that work and has been working wit them ever since."

"Well, how come I'm not locked up?"

"Simple, he's been giving them tha little niggaz, but now they want tha Big Fish."

"You know," Trap said pulling out his phone, "yo, where you at? Meet me in front of tha LQ on 2nd & DuPont in 15 minutes. Come on we bout to get to tha bottom of this Shit right now." Twenty minutes later, we were pulling up on 2nd & DuPont.

"What up yall?"

"Same Shit."

"I was gonna bring my whip thru today to have it detailed."

"So, what's up?"

"We bout to show you a whole nother side of tha game."

"That's what I'm talking bout."

"Let me make tha call to let them know we're on our way." The phone rang a few times and right when I was about to hang up Uncle Kev picked up.

"Talk to me nephew."

"We on our way up."

"OK. You know where to go, call me when you're done so I can send tha Clean Up Team."

"Gotcha, thanks again!"

"No problem at all. There's nothing more I like then to dispose of Rats!"

"We all set Cam, hit tha highway."

"Yo, can I spark this Shit up?"

"As long as it ain't no dirt."

"Dirt? I only smoke sour diesel."

"Light it up then."

"Naf, put that *'Know You Workin'* by Plies on."

"You must've been reading my mind." The whole time the song was on this nigga was rapping it word for word.

When it went off Cam said, "Play that back, niggaz need to take heed to some Shit."

"You ain't lying, niggaz a tell on they own mama to save they own Ass." We all just looked at this Snake Ass Nigga.

By the time, we got to our destination we were all high as an airplane. We all got up and walked inside the house which was really a sound proof arena for dog fights.

"What is this?"

"A dog fighting arena."

"We bout to watch a dog fight or something?"

"Nah, we came to take care of some very, very important bizness. Corey I've always treated you like a little brother long before you ever thought about tha game, haven't I?"

"Yeah, and I love for that."

"Do you Corey?"

"Of course, I do."

"Then why did you cross over?"

"What do you mean?"

"Tha Mafuckin cops!" Trap said now yelling with his .40 cal pointed at Corey.

"Whooa, whooa what you talking bout Trap?"

"Nigga you know what he talkin' bout. You lied about getting robbed for that half brick. We know you got booked so cut all tha you don't know what we talkin' bout Bullshit! We got people who know people."

"I didn't say nothing about you, I just gave them all tha Small Fish."

"You shouldn't have said Shit however it played out. You should have took it on tha chin like a real nigga."

"Trap I'm sorry," he pleaded with tears in his eyes.

"Save that Shit! It's fallin' on deaf ears. Have some Fuckin dignity and die like a man at least."

"This is gonna hurt me more than you," Trap said pulling the trigger until there were no bullets left.

"For good measures, Cam put one in tha center of his forehead like a prostration mark."

"Yo you a'ight?"

"I will be, lets bounce."

I hit Uncle Kev to let him know we were done.

CHAPTER 31

How Things Ended Up

Shelly ended up having a nervous breakdown and was admitted to the Terry Center.

Cam had a daughter by Angel and was still living a double life.

Lil kept trying to get Trap back to no avail because he was in love with Shonie.

As for me, I had my junior and opened a shop in Atlanta. This comes with ups and downs, but in the end, you have to ask yourself one important question! WHO CAN U TRUST?

ABOUT THE AUTHOR

My name is Jerz Toston and this is 2nd title. Betrayal & Deceit was my first one published and is available on all online bookstores.

I started writing books while I was incarcerated as a means to pass time, but soon realized that I not only had a gift for writing but also a passion for it. So, I continued to perfect my craft during my 60 months. This hasn't been an easy journey, but I wouldn't change a thing about it.